Inheritance

Inheritance

EVELYN TOYNTON

OTHER PRESS / NEW YORK

Copyright © Evelyn Toynton 2019

Production editor: Yvonne E. Cárdenas
Text designer: Jennifer Daddio / Bookmark Design & Media Inc.
This book was set in Mrs. Eaves
by Alpha Design & Composition of Pittsfield, NH

1 3 5 7 9 10 8 6 4 2

Library of Congress Cataloging-in-Publication Data

Names: Toynton, Evelyn, 1950- author.
Title: Inheritance / Evelyn Toynton.
Description: New York : Other Press, [2019]
Identifiers: LCCN 2018061174 (print) | LCCN 2019003440 (ebook) |
ISBN 9781590519226 (ebook) | ISBN 9781590519219 (paperback)
Subjects: LCSH: England—Fiction. | Domestic fiction. | BISAC: FICTION /
Contemporary Women. | FICTION / Psychological.
Classification: LCC PS3570.O97 (ebook) | LCC PS3570.O97 I54 2019 (print) |
DDC 813/.54—dc23
LC record available at https://lccn.loc.gov/2018061174

In memory of
ZPB, MD

Inheritance

A luxury weight-loss spa deep in the English coun-tryside . . . a country-house break to restore you body and soul." Rows of shiny machines in what was once the drawing room, barres on three walls of the morning room, black rubber matting on the study floor. Gray-painted walls, and all the furniture stripped out: the wing chairs, three-legged footstools, fringed sofas in tobacco-colored velvet. The paintings in their gilt frames, the clutter of books and lacquered snuffboxes on the parquet tables. The window seats have been removed, the fireplaces sealed up, the mul-lioned glass replaced with double glazing. And why should that matter to me, anyway, what difference can it possibly make now?

I remember her saying that when she was young she was always hoping she'd got things wrong, there was some explanation she hadn't thought of. "Because surely whatever it was couldn't be as awful as it seemed, or whoever it was couldn't have meant to be so nasty. I actu-ally thought that when I got older, and understood more, I'd see that everything was all right really. Oh dear." That's one of the phrases I associate with her: "Oh dear." Now I say it myself sometimes. When my baby daughter tries to walk and falls, "Oh dear," I say, scooping her up before she can start to cry, and she lisps it back to me.

I wouldn't have known if I hadn't picked up an old copy of *Vogue* at the hairdresser's in St. Paul. I was browsing through the magazines, waiting for my highlights to take, and there it was, a four-page spread complete with glossy photos. Women in identical quilted robes, with matching slippers, were gliding through the hall in single file on their way to the treatment cubicles in the basement. In the dining room, where they're served their penitential meals of kimchi and digestive bitters, the Hungarian naturopath who runs the place stood in the doorway, a model of Mittel-European chic with a faintly tragic air of wounded majesty. Another shot showed rows of padded pink lounge chairs on the terraced lawn, with the sun setting over the hill behind. Impossible to tell if the greenhouse to the left is still there, where, in her childhood, the body of a woman dangled from a hook.

The Duchess of Argyll Room, the Rosebery Room, the Mrs. Humphrey Ward: all the rooms upstairs, where the guests are housed, have been named for notable figures said to have visited in the glory days of Empire (the writer was careful to explain who those forgotten personages were). And each bedroom has been restored to an imagined former splendor, with a four-poster bed and a chaise longue, a ewer set in a flowered china basin on the bureau.

There was no mention of the nursery on the top story—the staff must be quartered there now—or her mother's lab across the hall, with its cages full of mutant rodents. In the nursery fridge, where Nanny kept the milk in summer, corpses lay on chipped Royal Doulton saucers, their paws in the air; these were the voles whose aberrant genes had been proved to account for their promiscuity.

The lascivious voles got a paragraph to themselves, but of course her mother's sex life was never alluded to. She was the heroine of the piece, the highborn Englishwoman, daughter of a lord, grown old in the house where she was born, but forging her own unorthodox path in the grand tradition of English eccentrics. A crusader for the environment, discoverer of new patterns in chromosomes. And there she was, her bony face staring out from under a jeweled turban, her hands clutching a Chinese walking stick carved with dragons. Even the great catastrophe of her final years, the article said, the death of her first-born child in a freak accident, had not crushed her indomitable spirit. "She died, aged 83, happy in the knowledge that her work was being carried on by others."

Her son and heir, the journalist explained, had sold the Hall to its present, corporate owners—a consortium in Luxembourg—after her death. "He is now living in Kenya, where, in his own way, he is continuing the family commitment to conservation, leading wildlife tours in the bush. When I finally reached him at the park lodge, he told me how glad he is that others can enjoy the tranquillity of his ancestral home." I must have given a snort, or muttered something under my breath; the stringy-looking woman opposite me, her head encased in an enormous puffy helmet, gives me a reproachful look. I roll up the magazine and jam it into my bag, but she isn't finished with me; she frowns her disapproval, shaking her head inside its bouffant covering. A staunch Midwestern moralist, who's never stolen even an old magazine. But instead of blushing, instead of removing the *Vogue* from my bag, looking sheepish, suddenly I'm furious. My hands are shaking, I glare at her so fiercely she averts her eyes, alarmed, pretending to examine the Redken poster on the wall. And still I can't let up, I'm glowering like a maniac, because she's all I've got, the only available target for my rage. Not one of its true objects is within reach, or ever will be.

Unlike her mother, she did not die happy. Stuff that in your pipe and smoke it, you stupid cow.

Part One

One

I had come to England, that May of 1986, expecting lofty and exalted feelings, but everywhere I went I kept picking up distress signals, thin vibrations of pain: a blotchy-faced girl shredding a Kleenex with both hands on the 73 bus, a dark birdlike man hunched over his soup in the shabby café near the South Kensington Tube station. And every morning, when I opened my eyes in my crummy hotel in Bloomsbury, all the mismatched bits of furniture bristled at me with silent malice. Then I'd tell them to fuck off, though not loud enough for them to hear.

On my eighth day in London, I woke to the smell of mildew: one door of the lopsided wardrobe had swung open during the night. I slammed it shut and padded to the window, peering through the net curtains to check out the street. Sometimes I'd stand for an hour, one leg snaked around the other, watching the people below. That morning it was drizzling, they were putting up umbrellas, tugging at their collars, tossing cigarettes into the gutter as they headed for the Tube. I couldn't pick out faces very well, but even from the third floor I could spot the luckless ones, trudging along with their heads down, communing with the sidewalk. A squat bald man barreled impatiently ahead, knocking his briefcase against a woman's bare legs. Ordinary, trivial rudeness. You'd have to be half nuts to get riled about a thing like that when it wasn't even happening to you. But there I was, heart pounding. Why should a dog, a horse, a rat have life . . . there was no answer to that, nobody had ever found an answer.

Time was running out. There were only a few days left to find the romance of England, in which I'd placed so much faith; so far it had eluded me even among the swans and turrets and purple irises of St. James's Park. It was just past nine o'clock. I made my way to the damp bathroom down the hall, where I brushed my teeth and splashed cold water on my face; back in my room, shivering by the tepid radiator, I dressed quickly in my good black suit and high heels, as though I had somewhere important to get to. In front of the cracked mirror of the wardrobe, I applied lipstick, blush, the new greeny-gold eyeliner in a pot that I had bought on the last day of my old life and never worn. Then I went down the shabby steps and onto streets newly washed with rain; in the first square I came to, the leaves on the trees were blurry with sunlit water. A tremulous, born-again feeling. I realized I was hungry, and climbed the majestic steps of the Hotel Russell.

A boy who looked no more than fifteen, in a maroon uniform whose matching hat tied under his chin with gold braid, emerged from behind a speckled marble pillar and asked if he could help. I'd like some breakfast, I told him. "Certainly, madam," he said, in a grave adult voice, though it squeaked. "I'll go see if we have a table available. Would you care to take a seat while you're waiting?" He gestured to a deep alcove at the left of the staircase, where a small round table with a vase of gold and crimson flowers sat between two identical plushy armchairs.

One chair was occupied by a bony old man in a clerical collar, with a rough-coated white terrier at his feet. As I seated myself opposite, he turned toward me, and I saw that the left side of his face had collapsed, his eye half-sliding onto his cheek. Very slowly, he lifted a trembling hand from the arm of his chair, then lowered it again. Men in suits and gleaming shoes walked past. A few minutes later my teenaged guide reappeared to inform me in the same grave voice that my table was ready. When I stood up the man opposite lifted his hand again, higher this time, so that I almost thought he was going to pronounce a blessing.

I ate a large plate of eggs and sausages and fried tomatoes in a cavernous room crowded with chandeliers.

After that I had a burst of determination; I got out my guidebook, with its little foldout maps, and made my way on foot to the National Portrait Gallery, where I tried to sort out which wigged and powdered man was which; I revisited the van Dycks next door; I wandered down the Mall and up Whitehall, and circled the thunderous-looking statues on plinths in Waterloo Place. Then I remembered that I hadn't yet been to Keats's house, and went looking for a 24 bus.

When I was eleven, my father had sat on my bed and told me the story of Keats's life in a voice husky with tears. At fifteen I had read Keats's letters in bed, under a pile of blankets, in a house my mother could no longer afford to heat, and believed that I could have saved him somehow. In college I'd kept on my desk a postcard of his grave that I'd found in an old library book.

I'd expected his house to be silent, like a shrine, but a straggly party of Russians was being ushered around by a stocky female with a harsh angry voice. I lingered on the ground floor, by the case with Fanny Brawne's engagement ring, waiting for them to go upstairs, but even when they did, I could still hear her booming away. The bony woman at the ticket desk told me that the Russians had gone to lay a wreath on Marx's grave in Highgate; now the guide was killing time before delivering them for their scheduled appointment at the Consulate. "She's come here before, she doesn't know anything about Keats," she burst out resentfully. "I think she just lectures them about the evils of the class system." I liked how fierce she sounded, like a dog growling; I wished I could go on talking to her—I hadn't heard my own voice much that week—but I couldn't think of anything helpful to say.

Upstairs the guide's guttural consonants followed me as I peered at the portraits, the death mask, the tiny bed he might or might not have slept in, trying to feel his presence in those white antiseptic rooms. Finally I gave up and took myself for a walk on the heath, where no nightingales sang, and one of my heels sank into a dog turd hidden in a clump of tiny purple flowers. But at least I hadn't picked up any signals of anguish from the Russians.

I had just made my way back to South End Green and turned onto Constantine Road when an unshaven man with half his teeth missing accosted me and asked if I could spare a couple of quid. "I could say it was for food, darlin', but I'm not going to lie to you." He winked at me. "I'm an alcoholic, see, I can't help it, it's a disease."

All I had in my wallet, apart from a twenty-pound note and a day's travelcard, was a five-pence bit and a few pennies—that and the ticket that allowed for free entry to Keats's house for a year, which he might not find very useful. So I handed over the change, apologizing: "I'd give you more, honest, but this is all I have on me."

"What about the note, then?" And when I said I wasn't going to give him twenty pounds he thrust his face at mine. "What's twenty quid to you compared to me? Eh?"

"Sorry." I closed my bag and walked away, but he followed behind, muttering just loud enough for me to hear, "Fuckin' Yank, we don't want you here, go back where you came from, foreign cunt," all the time breathing heavily, quickening his pace when I did. After a minute I was short of breath too—pant puff, pant puff: our breaths had synchronized—and hampered by my high heels, so that I could only trot in short steps. Across the street a woman was talking to her dog, a fat dachshund on a leash, without taking any notice of us. I wondered if I should shout for help, but I still hoped he was basically harmless, he'd get bored with calling me a Yank and a cunt and veer off.

Then he grabbed my hair, jerking my head back; I clutched my handbag to my chest and tried to hit him with my other hand, flailing behind me, while he tugged harder. At that point I did scream for help, but I had hardly gotten out the *H* when he let go, I heard a sort of crack, and turned my liberated head around: a tall sandy-haired man in a V-neck sweater had a cigarette in one hand and the other wrapped around my assailant's neck. "Now," he said, "I think that's quite enough, don't you? In fifteen seconds I'll let go, and then you'll scarper. Agreed? Just nod if you agree." Insofar as he could, the drunk nodded his head. "All right, off you go," Sir Lancelot said briskly, and released him.

"Fuckin' toff," the man said, rubbing his neck, and then, as he crossed the road, "Bleedin' imperialist toff."

"Thank you so much," I said. "Really, I can't thank you enough, you saved my life."

"I doubt very much that your life was in danger. Still, it must have been a nasty shock. You're not hurt, are you?"

"Oh, no," I said, "I'm fine," and burst into tears.

"Of course you are." He threw his cigarette in the gutter. "I was just on my way to the pub. You'd better come along."

I had to scurry to keep up as we headed back toward South End Green, which made me more teary. I must get rid of these shoes, I thought, sniffling, I must get some flats.

"Here we are," he said, opening the pub door, and I tottered after him to the long wooden bar, where he spent a good three minutes discussing what I gathered was soccer with the man behind it, while I diverted myself by reading the signs on the dark walls and the words on the little pumps.

Finally he turned to me and asked what I'd like to drink. He frowned when I said a gin and tonic, as though that was the wrong answer. But he went ahead and ordered it.

"Aren't you going to introduce me to your friend, Jules?" the barman said, measuring out the gin.

His eyebrows shot up. "I'm afraid we haven't been formally introduced." He turned to me again. "Would you mind telling us your name?"

So I did. "And you're Jules."

"Julian, actually. But Jules will do."

In a booth by the window, I got my first direct look at him: eyes the gray of rain clouds, a long bony nose, slightly jutting chin, an altogether decisive-looking face. He took a long swig. "So. Tell me what you were doing wandering around Constantine Road."

I had been to Keats's house, I explained.

"Ah yes. 'Hail to thee, blithe Spirit.'"

"That's Shelley."

"Christ, is it? You Yanks always seem to know more about English literchur"—pronouncing it in an exaggerated American accent—"than we do." His eyes strayed to the television in the corner, where a game of snooker was in progress. My feet were hurting, I was wishing I hadn't come. I decided to take a taxi back to my hotel. First, though, I would go to the ladies' room and tidy myself up. I was sure I had mascara running down my cheeks, and my hair felt greasy from the drunk's hands.

But when I stood up, he said gruffly, "One of my sisters was very keen on all that."

"All what?"

"Keats and Shelley and that lot. Byron. John Cam Hobhouse." I stared at him in puzzlement, not sure what this had to do with anything, or why he should sound so gloomy as he brought out the name of Hobhouse. Then his eyebrows went up again. "Don't look so gobsmacked. Why don't you sit down and finish your drink?"

So I did, and we exchanged some basic information: where I was from (I just said New York), where he was from ("originally the West Country"), what I did for a living (edit ecologically minded guidebooks for backpackers: I didn't say I'd quit my job). He told me he'd lived for a couple of years in Kenya; he and a friend of his who'd been born there had taken tourists on wildlife safaris. Once he'd been summoned to shoot a rogue crocodile that was attacking people. "Crocs are quite difficult to take out, actually, because you have to get them right in the brain, and they have exceptionally small brains."

"But did you manage it?"

"Afraid not. But at least he didn't kill me either. Would you care for another drink? You're looking much more cheerful, by the way. It must have been the croc." He waved away my twenty-pound note and went off to the bar.

What was he doing now, I asked when he got back. "You can't be leading safaris in London."

No, he said, he was your average disillusioned bureaucrat, not even a proper bureaucrat, because he worked for a think tank. "A ludicrous name for it, given the paucity of thinking that takes place there."

"But do you think?"

"Not very often. I'd be the office pariah if I did." He'd got a law degree at uni, he said; his remit was jurisprudence, exploring possibilities for coordinating sentencing guidelines among EEC members. He launched into a riff on the contradictory and byzantine laws governing sentencing in France and Italy and West Germany—"So you can get two years for passing a bad check in one country and six months for murder somewhere else"—breaking off occasionally when a shout or a wave of clapping alerted him that something had happened on the snooker table. Apparently there were great disparities in police procedures too, though those weren't his department. In France they never released a single fact about a crime until they'd arrested someone. In England they begged the public to help them, and all the mad people phoned in and told them how they'd seen the crime in a vision... strung... dem... The place was getting more crowded, there was much hooting and laughter; what with that and his accent and the two double gin and tonics I'd had on an empty stomach, I was missing about a third of what he said. Something about the SDP, something about the wankers in the government.

At one point I decided I'd better have something besides booze in my stomach, so I went to the bar and bought us two cheese rolls. By my third drink I felt sure that he was suffering, he was in pain without being able to express it. It made me very sad, so sad that twice I went to the ladies' room to have a little cry. In the passage leading to the ladies' room, there was a brown-and-white engraving of a lavishly mustachioed man, head of some Indian regiment, and as I leaned against the wall to steady myself and stared into his face, I realized that Julian's tragedy was that he'd been born into the wrong century: he was meant to be searching for the source of the Nile, or administering justice in some outpost of Empire. Protecting the women and children from rogue crocodiles. That made me cry some more.

I could never remember how I wound up going home with him that night—whether he said casually, with a shrug, Why don't you come back to my house?

or it was just taken for granted that I would. But somehow there I was, stumbling back along Constantine Road, bumping into him, until he turned right and I did too, down Rona Road, whose name I only learned later. I don't remember first entering the hallway of his house, or his first entering me, for that matter.

The next morning, though, I woke in panic, not knowing where I was. I heard his breathing next to me and jerked myself upright, staring around in the semidark to get my bearings. It was seven weeks and four days since my husband had dropped dead, and I was in a stranger's bedroom in London.

Someone was running down the stairs; I froze, waiting for a knock, but the footsteps continued down another flight, the front door slammed. For all I knew there was a wife somewhere. A child, even. He would want me out of there quickly. The best thing would be to escape before he woke, before things got awkward, and we had to extend this connection beyond its natural course. It used to happen in my single days in Manhattan, waking up next to some man whose name I wasn't sure of, while one or both of us tried not to show how badly we didn't want the other one there. Sometimes the man wasn't even polite enough to pretend.

Then came marriage to Eliot, who would never have wanted me to leave, who wanted to wake up with me every morning and keep me safe. But at some point an evil itch took hold of me; I sulked and snarled and banged doors and manufactured grievances. Trying to goad him into fighting back, wanting him to make me behave, so I could think of myself as nice again. Instead he followed me from room to room, pleading with me to be reasonable. On the second-to-last night of his life I'd stormed around shrieking that I was sick of him, I wanted out, and he said, "I curse the day I met you." He didn't know that nobody talked like that anymore. I laughed a snotty laugh, to escalate things. "Where did you pick up that phrase? In a romance novel?" Two days later, while he was talking on the phone in his office, a bubble that had lain dormant all his life burst in his brain.

He would have been horrified at my being there, not just the immorality of it but the risk I was taking. "Silly girl": he used to call me that, fondly; I liked it in the beginning and then I didn't. Now I heard his voice in my head, its flat Midwestern vowels, not bitter and accusing as I deserved but kind, sensible. It told me to gather my things, get dressed, get out: for all I knew the naked Englishman next to me could be a serial killer. (Eliot had also believed most Englishmen were gay, or at least bisexual. I could have gotten AIDS—it was the age of AIDS. Had he used any form of contraception?) I slipped noiselessly out of bed, furtive as a cat burglar, scooped up my clothing from the floor, wondering if I could find the bathroom without making a disturbance. I had no memory of where it was.

The curtains were drawn, the room was almost dark, but I could make out its size, about four times that of my hotel room, with high ceilings. I could just see his shape in the bed. There was a door to my left, slightly ajar, which I pushed open with the same stealth: sure enough, it was a bathroom, with a lovely big claw-footed tub, painted blue, with old-fashioned taps. I wished I could sink into it and shut my eyes, but I only dabbed at my sticky groin with the washcloth dangling over the side, threw some water at my puffy eyes, and dressed myself hurriedly, smoothing down the wrinkles in my black suit. After that I returned to the bedroom, to locate the door into the hall. And then a light switched on by the bed; he lay there watching me.

"Was it as bad as all that?"

"What?"

"The sex. Was it really that dire?"

I could see the light hairs glinting on his chest—a nice chest, taut and lean. It had been seven years since I'd been alone in a room with a naked man, except for Eliot, and he was running to fat. Despite my resolutions of a few minutes before, I felt a shameful thickening in my veins.

"I'm just a little embarrassed," I said, hovering.

"Well, don't be." There was a warning note to his voice, an I-will-not-put-up-with-any-silliness note, that brought me up short. My head felt very clear suddenly.

"Somebody just ran down the stairs."

"An old mate of mine who's been camping out in the loft for a few days. He has a heavy tread, doesn't he? But he's a decent chap."

Rain was splattering the windows on the other side of the room; the panes rattled as the wind struck them. The prospect of battling my way to a bus stop, getting soaked and splashed and whipped by gusts, the thought of the grayish light in my hotel room, the furniture bearing down on me: all that seemed too bleak to bear. Meanwhile the white, high-ceilinged room, with its tiny recessed fireplace surrounded by flowered tiles, its long, faded, chestnut velvet curtains, the oil painting of an old mill over the bed, felt like the very place I had come to find. This, finally, was England. And something about the crispness of his voice, his air of casual command: it seemed like a form of protection, there was so much certainty in it.

"Would you like a cup of tea?" When I nodded, he flung off the covers and stood up, taking a white cotton robe off the door and wrapping himself in it. I was left on my own, uncertain what to do: should I follow him downstairs? Should I sit on the bed with my suit on? I went to the window, pulling the heavy curtain aside, and stared out at the street. The rain had turned to drizzle, the sky was the colorless blank I would come to know so well, not even gray but a thick nothingness. After a few minutes I went down, I found my way to the kitchen, where he was pouring hot water into two mugs, and when we had drunk our tea and he had sworn at the toaster for burning what was meant to be breakfast we wound up back in bed.

Afterward he picked up the remote and switched on the dusty television balanced on the dresser opposite, hopping from channel to channel—not that there were so many of them, not half as many as in New York—making caustic jokes about the various dramas unfolding, until some politician appeared. Then he started shouting over the man's words: Liar! Ponce! Wanker! This state of emotional arousal only intensified at any mention of the prime minister: that bloody woman. Bloody bitch. Later he went out and bought not one but three newspapers, which he paged through, with more cursing, while I cooked us eggs and bacon in the kitchen, barefoot, wearing nothing but a T-shirt with a picture of a lion on it that he had dug out of a drawer for me. In the afternoon he watched a soccer game, while I flipped through the newspapers myself, reading the headlines and the book reviews. At intervals Eliot's voice still came through, but not as clearly, easier to shut out. I saw that it was possible to spend whole days with someone, in and out of bed, and never get close to knowing each other. Or even to feeling anything. It was bracing in its way, at least it held my self-pity in check, kept me from oozing.

"I'm a deeply shallow person," he said at one point, and I laughed appreciatively. And the next day, "I have such a very small heart—rather like a crocodile's brain—that anyone aiming at it tends to miss." I giggled. It was a relief to take my cue from him. Films and nuclear proliferation were perfectly fine topics of conversation. Mothers, fathers, old lovers might be alluded to in passing, part of some comic anecdote offered for the other's amusement, but the tone was kept light and droll, anything else would be out of line. Nor were there any of those drowsy postcoital confidences where you start rambling about watching a sunset from the top of a mountain, or how you felt when your dog died—or your husband, for that matter. (Remember, this was in a time before men started turning sensitive and emotionally aware. Especially English ones.)

He would seem to forget for whole hours that I was there, and then suddenly ask if I was hungry, or bored, or would like to go to a film. But the last thing I wanted was to leave the cocoon of that house. On Sunday night I made us a cheese omelet and opened a tin of sardines. On Tuesday I was due to fly back to New York. "I suppose they're expecting you back at work," he said, channel-surfing again. And when I shook my head, when I told him the job was finished, he said briskly, still clicking away, "Then why don't you just stay here?"

That shocked me: nothing had been said all weekend that implied a continuation; the whole mood of those three days was of a throwaway interlude. "Oh, I couldn't," I said. He didn't even answer, he kept his eyes on the television. But a moment after, the thought hit, Why not, why can't I? Nothing awaited me in Manhattan: I'd be camping on my pregnant friend Joannie's couch while I looked for a new job and a new apartment, with her husband interrogating her in the bedroom, in whispers, as to how long I'd be staying. And everyone I met asking questions about my life, my marriage. A few minutes later, with the BBC announcer talking about the new budget, I told him I'd changed my mind, I'd love to stay. "If you're sure that's okay."

"I wouldn't have asked you if it wasn't," he said coolly. No reassurances, or explanations either. Was it possible he was lonely? Or just tired of finding new women to sleep with? Maybe he had a thing for skinny blondes with brown eyes. Whatever his reasons, he had offered me a refuge, precarious though it felt, and I took it. On Monday morning, while he was off thinking in Westminster, I went to Bloomsbury, packed up my things, and returned to Rona Road in a taxi to start my new life.

Two

S he must want something," Julian said, when he told
me that his sister was coming for dinner. She was a
Latin teacher, he added, rolling his eyes, and frightfully soulful, too bloody sincere for words. Then he
sniffed, a sharp final sound. It reminded me of those
Englishmen in old war movies: "It's a bit of a bore"—
sniff—"but I'm afraid the Boche have just blown my
leg off."

Since the day I'd moved in, I had not so much as
shifted a magazine from one place to another on the
coffee table. Though I'd hung my clothes in one corner of the bedroom closet, and my nightgown stayed
under the pillow during the day, my makeup and
birth-control pills were still neatly zipped into my
toilet bag in the bathroom. It seemed important to do
nothing that looked like staking a claim.

But the thought of this sister of his looking me
over spurred me to assert myself. The day before she
was due, I walked up to Hampstead Village and bought
a Provençal-style cloth for the long pine table in the
kitchen; I replaced the motley assortment of objects
on the pewter hutch with some I had found shoved

into the cupboards below—a pair of heavy bronze candlesticks, some glazed Moroccan bowls, a bee-shaped honey pot of blue glass and etched silver that I polished and put in pride of place. The next morning I went shopping for food: a chicken, the ingredients for soup and bread and lemon meringue pie, my specialty during my marriage. And that afternoon I finally phoned my mother, to tell her where I was.

"Guess what!" I said, in the fakely chirpy voice I only ever used with her. "It looks as though I'll be staying in England a while longer!" I knew exactly where she'd be sitting, in the armchair opposite the television, wearing the green velour robe with the zipper that I'd bought her for Christmas four years earlier, with cold coffee in a white Snoopy mug on the little table beside her. She wouldn't have gone out for days, she probably hadn't been taking her hypertension pills and her antidepressants. But the two ladies from the church would drop by later, bringing cookies with brightly colored sprinkles, and make sure she was taking her medication. And then, on Monday morning, the social worker would come.

Eliot had been better at dealing with my mother than I was. He would tease her in a mildly salacious way, dreaming up all kinds of romantic adventures in her past; she'd toss her head girlishly, tell him to wash his mouth out with soap, clearly enjoying herself hugely. So I had dreaded having to tell her he was dead, I'd broken the news to her as gently as I could. But after a moment's silence, she only said mournfully that I was like her now, all on my own; I'd better be careful or I might wind up alone forever. "I saw Rita Mitchell last week. And you know what she told me? Her daughter's husband—they're down in Tennessee now—he's just been promoted to assistant manager. Some people get all the luck."

Now she said, "I never hear from your brother these days," not complaining really, just stating a fact, the way she stated so many other facts that happened not to be cheerful. I told her I would call him and get him to phone her, and then we said good-bye. She hadn't mentioned Eliot, dead for just nine weeks, but then I hadn't either.

He had prided himself on always being able to get taxis in the city; it made me sad to remember that, to remember his triumphant glance at me after his piercing whistle, the authoritative arm he shot into the air, had brought a yellow cab to a halt. Or what a point he made of finding interesting restaurants near us— not just Italian ones, but Korean and Moroccan and Ethiopian, he thought it would be such a treat for me, trying out exotic new dishes. But it wasn't enough, I could never care about it enough.

In his mind, I was some kind of exalted being, an unhealthy foundation for a marriage. I was "artistic," which he saw as meaning something inordinately deep: because I read poetry, instead of watching the Knicks with him on TV, I must be living on a higher plane. In all the years he'd been in New York, he'd only ever been to the Natural History Museum before we met; when I took him to MoMA or the Frick, or a foreign film, I think it satisfied some atavistic notion of Wife as a civilizing influence, in charge of a man's soul, while he went about the world's business. More than that, he was doggedly sure, based on two mediocre stories I'd published in the college magazine, that I was destined to be a great writer; over all my protests, he insisted that one day I'd be famous, and then he would be known as my husband.

He was unreasonably proud of me almost till the end, whereas I was never proud of him, not even of his earning power, impressive for the circles in which we traveled. He'd gone to law school at NYU, but quit to take over the failing business of the man he'd worked for during the summer after his first year; he was always having to deal with some emergency or other, a shipment that hadn't arrived, a consignment of the wrong goods. He prided himself on remaining calm in the face of his employees' panic. But in fact it was a slightly ignominious business: a factory in Long Island City that made not clothing but the price tags for clothing, those flimsy bits of cardboard attached to plastic strings. And it often teetered on the verge of bankruptcy. Not Master of the Universe stuff.

"Remember," his father kept saying on the phone, "you'll always be our daughter." His mother wanted me to come to St. Cloud and stay with them; she would send me a ticket, she said, while I sobbed on the other end of the line. I can't, I told her, I have to get far away, please try to understand, and she cried too, and said she did. I would sit cross-legged on the floor, the receiver pressed to my cheek, shaking with dread that one of them would say, You killed our son. But they thought my grief was as pure as theirs. They were going to erect a stone for him, they told me, Beloved son, beloved husband. It would say that God had called him home. He might not have minded that; he shared their weird innocence, an old-fashioned decency that could make me ashamed, make me feel cheap and sleazy and jaded, though in fact he was much better at navigating the world than I was. I got sidetracked by subtleties, peripheral things, and missed the obvious.

I packed up his things in a Gallo wine box—his diploma from Northwestern, the square black glasses I'd always hated (I bought him round tortoiseshell frames one Christmas, but he never had them fitted with lenses), the baseball he hit out of the park in Little League—and sent them off to Minnesota. I hauled his suits and shirts and ties, in garbage bags, and *Scott on Trusts* and the six volumes of Dumas Malone's *Jefferson and His Time*, to the Cancer Care Thrift Shop on Third Avenue, and sold the furniture to a junk dealer, and canceled the lease. I paid the super's junkie son to load up his father's van with boxes of my clothes and books and drive them to a storage facility in Yonkers.

His father had promised to wind up the business, warning me that it might not be worth much. But there were a few thousand dollars in our savings account, and the shares of John Deere that Eliot's grandfather had signed over to him on his twenty-first birthday. I knew I should give it all to charity, I had no moral right to it, but I wasn't as decent as Eliot, I cashed in the shares, I closed the account. I wrote a check for a thousand dollars to Save the Children and gave my wedding ring to a homeless woman slumped in a doorway on the corner. The next day I quit my job at the travel guide company and bought a ticket to London.

Now I was sitting in the front room of Julian's house, with Julian's sister telling me about her roses that were *sickening* and *dying.* No matter what she did she *could not* get rid of the brown spot on City of York. But just as she was leaving this evening, a neighbor of hers, who worked in the FO (whatever the fuck that was) had come over with a preparation she had made herself, that she swore was more effective than anything from the garden center. It had positively saved the life of her Arthur Bell, it had restored the glow to New Dawn. And it was so simple, that was the beauty of it: she just boiled up chamomile tea with stinging nettles. She would bring some over the very next day. Wasn't that terribly kind of her, Isabel said, smiling at me with queenly kindness herself. And though I thought she was completely phony, and possibly deranged, and almost wished she'd start asking me those searching questions about myself I'd been afraid a soulful, sincere person might ask—I simply could not get a foothold in this conversation, we seemed to be taking part in some play that she had the script for but I didn't—I couldn't help admiring her dress, a pale mauve jersey affair, with a high neck, sort of priggish really, but somehow it made me wish I were wearing a dress myself, instead of jeans and red boots and the V-neck velvet top I had bought at the Break shop on Rosslyn Hill. She wasn't wearing any makeup, either, not even lipstick, and she looked pure and radiant, like a Florentine Madonna, something by Filippo Lippi, only with faintly Slavic cheekbones. I'd been admiring my image in the bathroom mirror before I came down, thinking it subtly sexy; now I felt like trailer trash.

But that was nothing to the effect she was having on Julian. He was no longer the war hero but a character from a different bad movie, set in the prewar Balkans, a terribly urbane English diplomat with a silky line of patter, talking about stuff I'd never heard him express the slightest interest in before: some interior designer who'd died, whether the winner at Ascot had been pumped up with drugs. Then he got onto the story of how we'd met, in a superior, faux-witty style, as though it had all been too frightfully amusing—the drunk, the hair-pulling, the muttered references to toffs: "Rather outmoded, that brand of class warfare, I should have thought."

"And the irony was," I said prettily, because here at last was something I could say in the mode that seemed called for, "I was coming from Keats's house."

"Oh, poor you. It must have been horrid." The strange thing was, I felt she might really mean it.

"I would have given him the money," I said, anxious to clarify this point, "but all I had was a twenty-pound note and a few pennies."

"It's best always to keep some change in your pocket for those situations. Not that you should have to give them money, but..."

"It's what I did in New York, but somehow I didn't think about it here."

But Julian went on relentlessly with his monologue, in that same sneering, sub-Wildean style: the appalling claret served at a recent SDP function, which had given him such a splitting headache he'd almost decided to join the Tories; the friend from uni whose wife had run off with her father-in-law; what sounded like a very complicated and far-ranging scandal in Surrey, involving the passing of brown envelopes stuffed with cash between property developers and a high-ranking member of English Heritage. "We Anglo-Saxons," he said mockingly, "we've persuaded ourselves that corruption only happens elsewhere, we expect it from the Italians or the Africans, but we're meant to be superior to that sort of behavior, it's all honor and fair play with us. Which is exactly what enables it to continue undisturbed—nobody admits it's happening." And then, because she was silent, "Or don't you agree?"

"I don't know," she said slowly. "There must be all sorts of people who are trying to do the right thing, don't you think? Perhaps we just don't hear about them."

His whole facade wobbled for an instant, there was a flash of fear, before he rallied. "Of course it's different when you're wrangling with the ablative absolute all day. Much more satisfying, I'm sure."

"I really wouldn't know," she said. "I haven't *wrangled* with the ablative absolute in eons." Her voice sounded like Julian's a few moments before—like a wall of glass, nothing you could ever penetrate. Wow, I thought, she can do it too. Maybe they can all do it.

He yawned. "Sorry. I can't keep up with the hectic pace of change in your life." He looked at me. "Wasn't there some mention of our eating dinner tonight?"

We proceeded to the kitchen in silence, in single file, and I ladled the celery soup into bowls. "It's lovely," she said politely, though in fact it was too floury. She complimented me on the bread. "I'm afraid it's only soda bread," I said, with a little flutter of self-deprecation I thought of as English. "I'm cursed with bad yeast karma, it never seems to rise for me no matter how I cajole it. Very sad." An effortful smile from Isabel. She asked me where I was from in America. I told her, she said she didn't know it, was it very beautiful? It could be, I said, particularly in the fall.

"Oh, yes, I've seen photographs," she said. "The trees turn all those brilliant colors, it looks too too splendid."

I in turn asked her about her teaching, which turned out to be not at some high school, as I'd assumed, but at Kings College London. "And what about your book?" I asked then. "Do tell me about that"—another Englishism. Julian had said it was about dancing, making it sound like a how-to book about the polka, but it had something to do with dance and religion in the ancient world: "one of those books that nobody ever reads all the way through except the writer and the editor, and I'm not even sure about my editor." (Later I found out that wasn't quite true: the *TLS* had called it groundbreaking, the *LRB* reviewer used the word "seminal." She was way ahead of me in the self-deprecation department.)

Julian, who had sulked through the soup course, perked up when the chicken arrived, embarking, apropos of nothing, on a story about a chap he'd known who'd produced his English driving license in a car rental place in Florida and been asked by the woman at the counter what state England was in. America was a favorite topic of his; he would summon me from downstairs to watch with him if they were interviewing some obese John Bircher on TV, bitching about the Commies in the guvment fleecin' him to put food in the mouths of some lazy slut's bastards, or a preacher in Mississippi exhorting his followers to give him their dollars for the fight against homos. I sometimes wondered if the BBC had special scouts combing America for the most freakish specimens they could find; even in the bumfuck town where I grew up, there was no one to equal the grotesques on *Panorama*.

And still I would giggle merrily, eager to share the joke; I recited the Gurneyville cheerleaders' chants for his amusement, or the patriotic songs they made us sing at assembly: "I am so lucky to be in America"..."At 'em boys...give 'em the gun."

Not that night, though. Not with someone who said "too too splendid" and made me feel like a slut for wearing eye shadow.

But she hardly seemed to be listening; she kept darting troubled glances at the pewter hutch, her fingers in constant motion, kneading tiny bits of my soda bread on the new tablecloth. I couldn't understand why the sight of the innocuous objects on those shelves should distress her so, unless she coveted some family heirloom that had gone to Julian.

He had moved on to the subject of his work, describing his meeting about the prison bill with a committee from the House of Lords. "It's astonishing, really, that there's never been a revolution in this country. Half of them were barking mad, and the rest could charitably be described as clueless. One of them suggested we might introduce pigeon breeding into the prisons to build character. 'Give the poor devils something to keep them out of trouble, what?'" Meanwhile Isabel kept rolling those bread crumbs between her fingers, only smiling faintly in response. I could sense his irritation mounting, I thought we might be hearing about the ablative absolute again, so I jumped in, as falsely sprightly as I was with my mother: "Oh, that's perfect, I love that...I mean, they're real English eccentrics, aren't they? It just seems so right."

Then he said abruptly, "Speaking of barking mad, how's Sasha doing?" That was the sister he'd told me was bonkers, the one who knew about John Cam Hobhouse. When he'd announced that Isabel was coming, he'd said, "Not the mad one, the other one."

Her fingers stopped moving. "She's wonderful, actually. I mean, so much better, it's like a miracle, really. They say it happens like that sometimes, it can just disappear, the illness, when people get a bit older. Into their thirties. Though of course they can't be sure it will last. But then she's got this lovely young woman living with her, I'm sure that's got a lot to do with it. It makes such a difference, being able to have proper conversations again. Not being talked to as though she's an idiot. They have arguments about books, they go to the theater together, and to lectures at the V&A."

"How very jolly," Julian said, picking up his glass.

"You should really visit her sometime, Julian, I know she'd love to see you."

"Of course I'm going to visit her. I just haven't had time these past few weeks. We've been rather occupied here." He gave me a mock leer. "In fact I was going to ring her over the weekend."

"She'll be so pleased . . . Are you sure you have her new number?"

"Why don't you give it to me again, just to be sure? Not now," he said irritably, as she made a move to rise from the table. "Surely it can wait." And then, as she sat down again, "Relax. I said I'd go."

"I'll come with you if you want," I said.

"Ah, the famous magnanimity of women." He was pouring himself more wine; he didn't see her face as she mouthed a thank-you to me, the way it softened, as though she were suddenly shy. I felt different about her after that.

Throughout the evening, there'd been no mention of whatever it was she supposedly wanted from him. I thought my presence might be a deterrent, so when dinner was over I announced in something of Julian's manner that coffee would be served in the sitting room, and lingered in the kitchen long enough for the discussion to take place. But when I brought in the tray with the coffee, along with a pen to write down Sasha's number, Julian was telling yet another story, about an Irish chap in his office who'd crashed his Mini into a police van after a St. Patrick's Day celebration. Soon after that, she thanked us for a lovely evening and left. When I asked him what it was she'd wanted to talk to him about, he picked up the *Guardian* from the table and started leafing through it. "Nothing much." He turned a page. "It was to do with our diabolical mother, actually. Whose very efficient lackey she's always been." He replaced the *Guardian* on the table in favor of the *New Statesman*. "We had a sort of falling-out a few years back, and I cut the cord."

"What was the falling-out about?"

"I'd just as soon not discuss it, if you don't mind. It was a grueling enough evening as is, without an interrogation at the finish." He yawned. "Anyway, I'm knackered. Time for some telly. Shall we go up?"

"I've got to clear up . . . Why didn't you tell me how beautiful she is?"

"Perhaps because I knew you'd say it. Women always do. I don't think men fancy her much."

"How do you know? You're her brother, they wouldn't tell you if they did."

"She just doesn't look like the fanciable type to me. Besides, she never mentions a bloke, except her murdered Greek, and that was ages ago. I sometimes wonder if she might be frigid. Didn't she strike you as rather frigid?"

"What are you talking about? What murdered Greek?"

It was when she'd been on a fellowship in Athens, he said. "There was an uprising at the university there, they were protesting the fascist dictatorship, and the army broke it up with tanks. He was mowed down with some of the others, poor sod. So she came back to England with the kid."

"But that's horrible. How could you not have told me?"

"It was donkey's years ago. The daughter is fifteen now."

"You never even said she had a daughter."

"Forgive me, I had no idea you were so interested in my family history." Sniff. He put down the magazine. "One has to wonder what goes on under that facade of hers. Of course she presents herself as perfectly sane, the very model of self-containment. But that can't be all."

"What do you mean? Why shouldn't she be sane? You're pretty sane, aren't you?"

"Indeed." He heaved himself up. "Remarkably sane. Extraordinarily so. I learned it a long time ago. Now I really am going up, come join me when you're finished."

Twenty minutes later, when I went upstairs after dealing with the dirty plates and the leftovers and drinking the remainder of the wine straight from the bottle, he was lying naked on the sheets, channel surfing. But even once I'd washed off my makeup and shed my clothing I couldn't bring myself to join him. I stood fiddling with the light cord, trying to figure out what he'd meant about learning to be sane. "Did you ever meet him?"

"Who?"

"Her Greek lover."

He kept his eyes on the TV, where there was a program about sheepdog trials, with views of a castle in the background. "Once. In Athens. When I was traveling with my girlfriend from uni. There were a couple of others there too, the lot of them smoking like chimneys. But only tobacco. At first they all spoke English, for Deirdre's and my sake, but after a bit they were jabbering in Greek, getting very worked up. Probably about politics. And Isabel was hanging raptly on their every word, especially his; she seemed terribly proud of him, looking over at me to see if I was properly impressed, whereas he barely took any notice of her. Every once in a while he'd smile and nod in my direction, and ask some polite question, like what type of law I wanted to go into, and where were we heading next. And as we left he gripped me by the shoulders, he told me to get out of Greece, it wasn't a good place, I should come back when it was free. Then he quoted a Dylan song, about chimes of freedom. I remember that because it sounded so incongruous in his accent. That's all I can tell you." He switched off the TV and flung the covers back on my side, beckoning me to hop in.

"What about her daughter?"

"What about her?"

"You haven't even told me her name."

He shut his eyes. "Lucy Eleftheria. That means freedom in Greek. I told you, he was a revolutionary. She's quite earnest, like her mother, rather pretty though, she went off to boarding school in Hampshire this year, and I am extremely bored with this subject."

But even in bed, I couldn't stop thinking about her, bits of the evening kept coming back to me, making me wince with shame. Because I knew how we must have seemed to her, Julian with his glib patter and me doing my cheap little imitation of English gentility. I have to explain, I thought, I have to tell her, though it wasn't clear to me what exactly I would tell—the truth, the whole ball of wax? Did I think she could grant me absolution? Meanwhile our bodies were going through their usual contortions, though even when desire kicked in, the heat of it couldn't stop my brain from ticking over: I felt more than ever how separate we were from each other, two lonely animals clambering over each other in a pretend act of love.

While my limbs accommodated him, while I rocked him inside me, I was feverishly hatching plans. It was like being in high school again, working out schemes for waylaying the long-haired boy from civics class I'd spotted with a copy of Baudelaire. We'll go and see Sasha, I thought, then I can call her up to report, and the idea pleased me so much I almost laughed with gladness. Later I would say it must have been a premonition, but at the time it felt more like nostalgia, to do with the past and not the future—a reminder of some other way of being I'd forgotten about, a sliver of myself I thought I'd lost for good.

Three

In my last year at Stony Brook, I began to believe—mistakenly, as it turned out—that I had it in me to write a novel, and signed up for a creative writing course with an aging novelist from Kentucky, author of several books about Appalachian rednecks, who shut his eyes and rocked back and forth, all but groaning audibly, as we read our stuff aloud in class. He also said "fucking" a lot, which he seemed to think would shock us.

He didn't say my nascent novel was fucking boring, as he'd told the student who read before me; he said I had a fucking unreliable narrator and didn't seem to know it: "It's okay for Clara not to see her father was a prick for walking out like that, but we've got to know that you see it." Clara was my middle name; the father in the book was called Peter, which was my father's. Much of my reason for writing the book was to make the world see that he wasn't a prick after all. My mother thought he was, the welfare officers did, and the ladies from the church. I had set out to show they were wrong.

Even when we sat around the dorm at night, ruthlessly dissecting our parents' failings, I could never bring myself to condemn him. (My mother was a different story.) Instead I painted him as the principled rebel he had almost been: the only teacher at the high school who'd refused to sign the loyalty oath (in fact he'd caved in at the end; he'd been fired not for subversion but for drunkenness), a man who had thrown off the shackles of his dead marriage, his dead-end job (the shoe factory in town had taken him on after the Board of Education let him go), a man whose talent had been thwarted by the narrowness of his milieu. Because my father too had written fiction.

But like the Kentuckian, Eliot found that version of things unacceptable. To him my beloved father, who'd sung me arias and recited poems for me, who'd woken me up to look at a harvest moon, was nothing but a deadbeat and a weakling. I had to stop deceiving myself, no man had the right to walk out on his children, he said, with such finality it felt as though the moral failing was mine as much as my father's. No wonder, then, that during my marriage the novel withered and died. Though Eliot was certain I would write something wonderful, though he urged me never to give up ("a quitter never wins and a winner never quits") and bought me a beautiful red fountain pen and a green gooseneck lamp for my desk, secretly I blamed him for my lack of progress: before my book ever had a chance, he had strangled it with his deadly common sense. Now that he was dead, now that I was living on his money in another man's house, with nothing else to do, I felt I owed it to him—idleness being against his principles—to revive it in his terms, a story of a feckless father and a pitifully deluded young girl pining for his return. But I couldn't seem to strike the right note.

Instead I used the red pen to write false lying letters to his parents. Julian didn't exist in those accounts of my London life; I was still in my hotel room, I was thinking of them and of Eliot. I borrowed sentiments from sympathy cards with flowers and ribbons on the front: I hoped they were finding comfort in their happy memories, in knowing how much Eliot had loved them. Knowing he hadn't suffered. That he'd been happy. (That was the worst lie of all.)

Not even to Joannie, my best friend in the city, did I admit my true situation. I read about exhibitions in the paper and described them to her, I dug up facts of interest about historical sites I hadn't visited, I asked her to send me pictures of her pregnant stomach, which she duly did. I'd been having lunch with her at a Thai restaurant on Mott Street while they were trying to resuscitate Eliot at the hospital in Flushing; by the time I got back to my office and got the message from his assistant, he'd been dead for fourteen minutes.

The letters tucked in my bag, I would leave the house, delaying my return from the post office by heading up Rosslyn Hill to browse in antique shops, clothing shops, bookshops, loitering behind shelves and among racks of dresses to eavesdrop on people's conversations. There were none of the bald direct statements, the kind of forceful opinions, that everyone went in for in Manhattan. The style was different, the cadences were different; the rule seemed to be that complaints, about the weather and every other subject, must be leavened with wry jokes and end on a note of optimism. ("Never mind. Perhaps it'll brighten up this afternoon.") I was very pleased with myself when I managed to bring off what seemed like the authentic tone, and, echoing Isabel, I started using the word "lovely" a lot.

One afternoon when it had failed to brighten up I decided to make use of the lovely feather duster I had bought in a junk shop in Flask Walk, a plumy Edwardian-looking thing with a long handle—the cleaner who came every Wednesday morning, a tiny shy Indian woman, confined herself to mopping and vacuuming and wiping off surfaces in bathrooms and kitchen. I began on the books in the study, all those dreary-looking law textbooks and memoirs by Labour politicians; after that I climbed on a chair to get rid of the cobwebs on the moldings in the front hall. Then I decided to dust the pictures.

I had dusted my way through the living room, with its photographs of lions and its gilt-framed painting of a cart and horse; the conservatory, with its framed Pink Floyd posters; the Claude Lorrain prints of lakes and mountains, in many shades of brown, in the study. I was humming to myself as I worked my way up the stairs, brushing the cobwebs off a lithograph of a red flag with Arabic lettering, a painting of a coffee cup on wood, a photograph of Einstein sticking out his tongue. Second from the top was a framed pen-and-ink drawing I'd never noticed before, of a vast house with a fountain in front, and oriel windows and many chimneys. It was so covered with dust that I took it down to blow on it, rubbing the glass with the heel of my hand, and saw the inscription at the bottom: Sidworth Hall, Teign Valley, Devon, 1979, with a printed signature, all in capitals, in the right-hand corner: SASHA DENBY.

"The West Country," Julian had said when I asked where he was from in the pub that first night, conjuring up some wild rocky place in my mind, nothing like the dream landscape my father had promised to take me to the summer he left us, to show me the pink and white flowers in the hedgerows.

My father never talked about D-Day, or the Battle of the Bulge; only much later did I think to wonder what happened to him on those beaches, or afterward, in the forests of the Ardennes. It was always Devon he wanted to tell me about, those nights he came into my room and sat on the bed, sipping from his glass of Scotch—the thatched cottages, the wild ponies on the moor, the woods full of bluebells. The last days of his innocence.

"You'd love it, kitten, you walk through the countryside, and off on a rise, or in a little dip, you see this old stone church, it might be hundreds of years old, a thousand years, and there are sheep grazing in front...and crooked stone walls everywhere, straggling up the hillside, and birds singing their heads off.

Actual nightingales, I always thought they were like unicorns, they didn't really exist, but they do, they've got 'em... and the villages have these crazy names, like Warrington Beefstock and Gormsley Pudge... and everywhere is so green. So green you can't imagine." I'd fall asleep listening to him talk about the nightingales and the sheep and Gormsley Pudge. "Someday I'm going to take you there," he'd say, but it was always someday, a promise for the future, until that last spring, when school was almost out, and he came into my room and said, "Tell me, Miss Devereaux, what are your plans for the summer?" I looked at him, puzzled, and he took my hand, gripping it hard.

"I shouldn't tease you... because I've been thinking, listen, I want us to go to England. I want to show you Devon while you're young enough for magic." Other plans had been hatched on those Friday nights when he'd been listening to records in the basement, only to dissolve into nothingness by Saturday morning. But he was looking at me so intently, with such eagerness, I couldn't disappoint him. In some ways he was younger than I was, I knew that even then. I knew, too, that other people saw him as not the right kind of grown-up; only the week before, when two girls from my class came to the house, and he was playing Count Basie for us, I caught them rolling their eyes behind his back: "Listen to this," he was saying, "this is a great part, you have to listen," while they smirked knowingly at each other.

"Oh, please," I said, "please let's go." And then

he was gratified, he chuckled, and squeezed my hand against his cheek. "You're going to love it," he said, "I promise you." We could stay with his friends the Crofts, he said, his friend Stan, who had been with the British Army, helping to train the Yanks...

My mother must have protested, but not with any real force; she had reached the point of aggrievement then where it seemed her sole aspiration was to martyrdom; everything he said evoked sighs and grimaces. The very next week, he took me, full of importance, to Mr. Sansom on Main Street to have our passport photos taken; Mr. Sansom, too, he told about the churches and the sheep. But by the time the little blue-and-gold booklets arrived in the mail, he was gone.

For all those months that my mother and the welfare people and his boss at the mill were speculating angrily about his whereabouts, I was sure he was in Devon, among the nightingales. But however much it hurt that he'd left me behind, I stayed loyal, I never told a soul. Only years later did I realize that he couldn't have left America, his passport hadn't arrived yet when he left.

The night before he disappeared, another Friday, he came and sat on my bed just as I was falling asleep. He sounded different from the way he usually talked to me, almost as though I was his own age. "Hey, Annie"—not baby, or kitten, or Miss Devereaux—"did I ever tell you about Marty?" I shook my head. "He was my buddy in the platoon. A Jew from Brooklyn. We used to hang out together a lot. He was always teasing me about the stories I published in the base paper. 'You gotta stop with the Hemingway crap,' he'd say, 'that shit's passé now.' But he told the other guys how terrific the stories were, he said they should remember my name, I'd do something great one day."

I had always felt, always known, that he was special, different, better than my mother and everyone else we knew. Now I had proof.

"Could I read them?"

"Oh, sweetheart"—I was back to being a child again—"they were no damn good. Marty was right, I was trying to be Hemingway."

"Are you still friends with him?"

"Who?"

"Marty."

He took a long swig of Scotch. "Marty's dead, kitten. Blown up the minute we hit the beaches." He patted my hand. "You'd better get some sleep, it's late."

The next day, he was gone. And shortly before I left myself, to go to college, I went through the boxes in the garage where my mother had stowed his things and found, buried beneath a jumble of old belts and shirts and his prize collection of Bix Beiderbecke 78s, two moldy copies of the base paper with his stories in them, along with half a dozen unpublished ones, in faded blue type on carbon paper. Maybe he'd sent the originals off to magazines he hoped would publish them. Even I could see that Marty was right: they were tough-guy, mock-Hemingway stuff. He'd been twenty-five, twenty-six when he wrote the last ones,

going on the GI Bill to St. Lawrence, where my mother
was a secretary to one of the deans. Maybe if she hadn't
gotten pregnant, if he hadn't taken on the teaching
job and the mortgage and all the rest of it, he would
have kept at it till he found a voice that was his. Maybe.
It was even possible that one day a package would arrive
at our house, a shiny new copy of his Great American
Novel, and he would be transfigured in everybody's
eyes, they would all admit they'd judged him unfairly,
he'd been a great man all along. But only possible
in the sense that anything was possible. Even then, I
couldn't muster up much hope.

Four

It must say something about my relation to reality that I had never tried to locate Devon on a map. But I had noticed, in Julian's study, a *Times Atlas* jutting out from the top shelf, which I now took down and opened to a map of the British Isles. And there it was, my lost Eden, in the bulge of the jagged peninsula tapering off to the west. Devon. The West Country.

I foolishly supposed that Julian would be as pleased as I was over my discovery. Finally I would tell him the whole story of my father's desertion, and the aborted trip to Devon, and he and I would go there, he could show me all the places my father had described. After that things would be different between us, we'd have found our connection.

Except I never got to tell my story. As soon as he returned home I began, excitedly, to explain about finding the drawing, I thought of that as the preliminary part, to be hurried over, but he cut me off: "Where is the bloody thing? What have you done with it?" And when I told him it was in the study, with the atlas, he brushed past me and came back holding it away from him; he marched out the front door and left it propped against the dustbins. "I'd forgotten it was there," he said grimly when he came back in. "I would have got rid of it ages ago."

"But why? Isn't it the house you grew up in?"

"It is. Which is precisely the reason I got rid of it. You have answered your own question. Well done. Now shall we go to the pub? It's snooker night, remember?"

That Sunday, though, by prearrangement, we went to see the drawing's maker, at the flat in Elm Park Gardens where their mother had installed her.

"She seems very taken with her new nanny," Julian had said when he got off the phone with Sasha. "Everything is referred back to her—we're to be given tea by Daphne, Daphne is so looking forward to meeting us, et cetera." I really expected Daphne to be like a nanny, stout and motherly, but in fact she was a slight young woman with a Dutch-boy bob and a shiny face. I wondered if she was a Quaker, if she had taken on this job in the spirit in which someone else might join the Peace Corps.

She ushered us into a pale gray room where Sasha waited on a pale green sofa, looking like a parody of normalcy, the picture of Blandly Average Womanhood in an avant-garde play: dumpy, secretarial, in drip-dry brown trousers, a beige blouse, a brown cardigan; her short brown hair was permed, her blue eyes almost hidden in little rolls of shiny-smooth fat. Isabel had said she was longing to see Julian, but she stayed put when we entered, she didn't even reach up and put her arms round his neck as he bent to kiss her. Instead she clenched her jaw, turning her face away, so that the kiss landed on her hair. There was a mottled red flush on her cheeks that remained the whole time we were there.

Having taken our coats and seen to it that we were seated, Daphne excused herself to go prepare our tea. "Give a shout if you need any help," Julian said. He had not yet addressed any remarks to Sasha, beyond Hello.

"So you're from America," she said to me, in a high, aggressively bright voice, full of barely concealed rage. I couldn't tell if she hated me for being Julian's girlfriend or if she was taking her revenge on him for staying away for so long. "Aren't you lucky. I adore America. I'd love to live there."

"Are you sure about that?" Julian asked mildly. "I seem to recall you were only there once, for about a week, when you were twelve."

She didn't even look at him. "I have the most glorious memories of it. And of course I see it all the time, in the cinema. I love the way Americans smile, with all their teeth showing. Though you're not smiling. What are you doing in this country, anyway? I mean, apart from fornicating with my brother. What made you come here?"

It did not seem like the time to tell her about Eliot, or my trip with my father. So I said feebly that I had always had a thing about England.

"Really. How odd of you. What sort of thing?"

Oh well, I said, trying for lightness, I guessed it had started in earnest when I read *Jane Eyre*.

"Yes? And what else?"

Well, and the rest of English literature, I said, feeling increasingly foolish.

"Such as?"

Such as Keats, I told her, and Coleridge, and George Eliot, and Wordsworth, and Virginia Woolf.

"I see. So you're here because of a lot of dead people, is that right?"

I supposed so, I said.

"That's not awfully healthy, you know. You could wind up very very unhappy if you go on like that."

On the contrary, I said recklessly, my relationships with dead people had given me some of the happiest times of my life.

She looked at me in triumph. "Then you really shouldn't have come. Because, you know"—she leaned toward me—"*they're not here anymore.*" After that she turned her attention to Julian, telling him about a dream she'd had, in which they'd been skiing down a slope together. "Do you remember that time in Pontresina, Junes? That awful instructor with the wart on his nose? Was he actually called Adolf, or was that just our name for him?" She and Daphne were planning to go to Italy that winter, she said, maybe to Umbria. Then she said abruptly, "You haven't told me what you think of my new digs. Would you care to see the rest of it? I'm thinking of redecorating, I don't like all these *calming* colors. What do you say? Wouldn't this room look better in shocking pink?"

"That sounds delightful," Julian said, drawling out the word, and she stuck out her tongue at him just as Daphne reappeared, bearing a lacquered tray with a teapot and cups and little iced cakes, which she set down on the low table by the couch.

"So did Isabel make you come?" Sasha asked him, over Daphne's head. "Isabel comes to see me all the time. Isabel the Good. We're like some allegorical figures in a medieval painting, Issy and me, a tree full of red berries, with the good sister on one side and the evil one on the other."

"I thought we'd agreed you weren't going to talk like that anymore," Daphne said gently. "You remember what we decided about evil." She held up the sugar bowl, which had little peasant figures painted on it in red and blue, and asked if we took sugar.

"You're getting confused," Sasha told her. "It was Issy you decided it with. My theological sister. Not me. Anyway, he knows what I mean, don't you, Junes?"

"I wish you'd stop calling me that," he said calmly, taking the cup and plate Daphne held out to him. She had already given me my tea and cake.

"Well, I'm *sorry*. I do apologize." Her glance shifted to me. "Why aren't you eating your cake?"

"I was just about to."

"You must eat it, it was bought specially for you. For your visit here today." She watched while I took a bite. "Now you have to tell me it's delicious."

"It is. It's very delicious."

"Extremely so?"

"Yes, extremely."

"Good. Though the nutritionist says sugar is a depressant, I have to eliminate it from my diet. Not because it made me fat, either, because it didn't. It's the meds. They put little globules of fat in those pills, to puff out your cheeks, so you can't have sex."

Meanwhile Julian was talking to Daphne, who had seated herself on a low chair in the corner. "How did you get into this line of work? Do you have a degree in psychology?"

"No," Sasha said loudly. "In English literature. Like your girlfriend here. Only Daphne went to UCL, and Annie probably attended...I wouldn't like to guess. Some of those American universities have the most extraordinary names, as Mum might say. 'What an extraordinary young man...what an extraordinary idea.' You see how it's done. What she really means is 'Sasha, you worthless cunt.' It's quite simple once you get the hang of it." She smiled kindly at me. "I used to be literary myself, you know, I was always declaiming poetry to the dogs. Lord Byron was my passion. But now I'm like Mr. Brooke, in *Middlemarch*—remember what he used to say, how he went into all that at one time, but he saw it wouldn't do? That's exactly right: I saw it wouldn't do. Now I confine myself to Joanna Trollope. Better than diazepam. Better than ECT even. Good. You've eaten all your cake. I hope you don't think my brother actually loves you, that would be too pathetic." And to Julian, "But they're always a bit pathetic, aren't they, Junes? I mean, the ones I've met. Of course there could be others who were real tigers, I wouldn't know about that."

"All right, that's enough," Julian said, getting to his feet. "Time to go." He turned to Daphne. "Thank you for the tea." And because I went on sitting there, blinking, "Come along. We're leaving now." I rose and followed him, making little noises of embarrassment at Sasha, who ignored them; she was rocking back and forth on the couch, humming loudly. Now I can't phone Isabel and report, I thought miserably. She might even blame me for things going so wrong.

Daphne followed us into the hall. "I'm so sorry. I'm sure it won't be like this the next time you come."

"Nothing to apologize for. I'm used to it."

"It's just unfortunate that you caught her on a bad day." But by that time we were on the stoop, and he was ushering me down the steps; he pretended not to hear. For a minute we stood on the pavement; the sun was just beginning to set, the sky was a clear darkish blue over the orderly line of white houses. I almost said, "I love this time of day in London," but that was too inane, while anything more real seemed freighted with danger. I hung back for a moment, afraid he might touch me. Once again, the little game we played, as though we were an actual couple, had been upended, the pieces were scattered all over the board.

Even Julian may have felt it. He was unusually silent, getting straight into the car, staring straight ahead while I arranged myself on the seat next to him. We drove off through the leafy, peaceful streets, and then through Knightsbridge, past the Brompton Oratory, Harrods, Harvey Nichols, the silence extending itself past the point where it seemed rescuable. By the time we reached Hyde Park I had tried out a dozen possible lines in my head and rejected them all. Then I came up with one that seemed safely neutral. "It's strange how the three of you look so different."

"Why? Do you look so much like your brother?"

"Yes, as a matter of fact. A lot like him."

"Well, aren't you the lucky one. Or, excuse me, should I say he is."

We went sailing past the Wellington Arch, which even then, with the atmosphere in the car coagulating by the minute, gave me a secret thrill, a sense of grandeur that I could not connect to the evils of imperialism.

Finally, when we were stopped at a red light on Edgware Road, I took a deep breath and said, "She's sick, you know that."

"She's also exceptionally nasty, in case you didn't notice. I didn't much care for the way she treated you. Or the way you crawled to her, for that matter."

"I wasn't crawling. I was just trying to be polite."

"Rubbish. You were positively obsequious."

I told myself he was upset, he was simply taking out his wounded feelings on me. His hands on the steering wheel were trembling slightly. But it seemed he had only begun. He glanced over, shifted gears, shot forward. "Of course you're like that with anyone English. The people whose country it really is. Even at the pub the other night, you had to step aside and let those two little tarts walk in ahead of you. As though to assure everyone that you're not one of those aggressive Americans, not you, you know your place."

It was such an unexpected line of attack that I almost had to admire it. I filed it away for future consideration, while saying in my snottiest voice, "It doesn't take a shrink to figure out the connection between that outburst and what just happened. If you're angry about the things she said, I don't blame you. But don't take it out on me. Now, do you want to talk about it or not?"

"What is there to talk about? My sister is a mad bitch, full stop. And you chose to pander to her. I think we can dispense with the amateur psychology. Though I realize it's your national religion. The American creed."

"What's that supposed to mean?"

"Sorry. Mustn't be opaque. Must remember who I'm talking to. You seemed about to trot out that revolting phrase the Yanks use. Getting in touch with one's feelings. Isn't that it? Which I'm not really in the mood for right now."

"Fuck off."

"I merely wanted to clarify. Tell me, is it your father that you and your brother jointly resemble? The departed Mr. Devereaux? Or his madam? And what was Mrs. Devereaux's maiden name? Thibodeaux?"

"Let me out of this car."

"Don't be ridiculous. We'll make our way back to Rona Road, where you can pack your belongings if you like, and flounce out in style."

But when we arrived, the skinny, harried-looking woman from next door, whom I'd exchanged occasional smiles with by the gate, was standing on the street with her two small sons, having locked herself out. "So stupid of me," she said helplessly, without much conviction, as if she wasn't really surprised. "But would you mind if I used your phone for a minute? I want to see if a friend of mine can put us up until the locksmith in Gospel Oak opens again tomorrow."

Julian gave her his most charming smile. He had a better idea, he said; they should come inside while he phoned around for a locksmith who worked on Sundays.

"Oh, how kind of you. You're sure it's not too much trouble?"

"No trouble at all." I settled her and the children in the front room and went to make tea and fetch the milk and chocolate digestives. Julian was pacing around the kitchen with the phone to his ear. "I'm talking about a single mum with two kiddies, mate, and you say in your advert you provide twenty-four-hour service. Let's think about that for a moment, shall we? I presume you know there are laws about false advertising." Even to me he sounded impressive, a bully in a righteous cause. "You can charge me whatever you want. Just get here. Within the hour." He gave the address, made the man on the other end repeat it, hung up as I was piling the tray with the tea things and Cokes and biscuits, and took it from me.

Together we soothed the woman, assuring her we didn't mind a bit, and tried to divert the children. Julian asked which team they supported, and teased them about the departure of someone named Frank. By the time the locksmith arrived, sporting a blue Mohawk and multiple piercings, and we had waved them off, the woman still offering fluttery thank-yous and prodding each boy to thank us in turn, it was somehow impossible to rekindle the fight, though we didn't look at each other either. He turned on the radio news, and after a couple of minutes I ostentatiously picked up my Anita Brookner from the living room table and marched off to the conservatory. But I couldn't concentrate on the tangled relationships in the medical library. I thought about going to a movie, any movie, just so he'd wonder if I was coming back.

Then I remembered I'd been going to phone my brother, to tell him to call our mother. And suddenly I badly wanted to hear his voice.

Once I had felt closer to him than anyone. We used to huddle by the boiler in the basement when our mother was asleep, planning our escape from Gurneyville. He was going to be an artist; he would show me his drawings, and I always said they were brilliant, though I couldn't tell if they really were. He was going to live in Paris when he left home—we were so naive we thought Paris was still where artists lived—and work on his paintings until he was discovered. For his birthdays, and for Christmas, I would give him books on Rembrandt or Vermeer, or Winsor & Newton paints I'd bought with my babysitting money.

On the wall of our living room in St. Paul is a framed drawing of a woman in a medieval headdress, a copy he made of a Holbein, from one of the books I gave him. It must have been one of the last drawings he made, because around the time I went off to Stony Brook he stopped doing art and took up drugs instead. The night I came home for Thanksgiving he went out with his friends after supper and was still not back at midnight; even on Thanksgiving, after the ritual meal, with the donated turkey and the sweet potatoes mashed up with marshmallows, these mysterious friends of his showed up at the curb in their car, honked the horn once, and waited for him to emerge; they never came to the door. "Just some guys," he said, when I asked who they were, and my mother, when I questioned her, only shook her head resignedly. "At least he's not up in his room all the time, playing that thumping music."

Every night I waited for him in the living room, and as I rattled on, trying to engage his interest, he edged his way toward the door, smiling a vague polite smile. I wanted to know if he had a girlfriend, or maybe he'd discovered he was gay, but first I had to win him back. I told him about my roommate, who was very homely, but obsessed with her appearance; she applied face masks every night, she read *Vogue* and *Harper's Bazaar* and hardly ever went to class. I told him about my Contemporary Novel professor, who wore his shirts opened almost to the waist, and soft suede boots almost to the knee, and gazed out the window in silence for a moment at the beginning of every class, before making some musing remark about the nature of time. "Honestly, you can't imagine what a pretentious jerk he is," I said, with more animus than I really felt, while Adam went on grinning at the air. I heard myself babbling on, I knew I was boring him, but I couldn't shut up. And finally, having inched his way across to the hall door, he'd say he was wiped out, he had to get to bed.

He looked younger than when I'd left, his skin so clear and milky it seemed impossible that he ever needed to shave. He looked, in fact, like the eight-year-old I used to take by the hand and walk down to the stream to watch the kingfishers in the days before our father left. It must have been the drugs that were smoothing him out, though I didn't know that then. He'd just stand there smiling as though at some private joke as he sidled away.

I decided he was angry at me for going off to college and abandoning him, that he was punishing me with silence. The last morning I was home I went and knocked on his door, and though he didn't say Come in, only asked Who is it?, I opened the door and walked in anyway. He was lying in bed, not smiling for once; he seemed cross at me for interrupting whatever he was doing, which appeared to be nothing.

"I feel bad," I said, which was true, but my voice was false, because it was such a conscious effort to break through. I sat on the end of his bed, as I had a thousand times, though now I felt like an intruder. "I'm leaving today, and I've hardly even seen you; we haven't really talked."

"Don't feel bad," was all he said. He plucked at the bedclothes, averting his eyes from me; he kept bunching up the sheet between his fingers and then letting it go again and starting over.

"But I do." I took a deep breath and went on, with the same false directness. "How are you, Adam? I wish you'd tell me."

"There's nothing to tell. I'm fine. A little tired right now, that's all. But fine. Don't you worry."

"How are things at school? How's Mrs. McGrath?" She was the art teacher at the high school; she too had encouraged him, had even invited him to her house sometimes on Saturdays, and shown him the postcards she and her husband had brought back from their trips to Italy.

"She's okay," he said, still without looking at me. "She's fine."

"Have you been doing any new drawings?"

"Not really . . . I'm sort of taking a break from art, you know? Just for the time being. Thinking about what I'm going to do next."

"Okay. But I hope you'll get back to it soon. You've got a real talent; you've got to do something with it."

"Oh, yeah. Yeah. I will. You don't have to worry about that." Now he looked up; I could tell he was willing me to go.

"You just don't seem very happy, that's all."

"Actually," he said, and laughed loudly, "actually, I've never been so happy in my life."

"Okay, then. I didn't mean to pry. I just need to know you're all right. I love you, you know that."

"Sure," he said, but he didn't say he loved me too. He had a sly look to him then, as though he were laughing at me, which he probably was. A year later he dropped out of high school and went to live in a fifth-floor walkup on Fifty-Sixth Street and Ninth Avenue in Manhattan, with a bathtub in the kitchen. When I took the bus down from Stony Brook to see him, there were needles lying in plain view on the counter; he went out a few minutes after I arrived, and didn't come back. A few months after that he disappeared, to resurface in Pittsburgh, where he worked in a video store—cum—head shop and took up tantric yoga. The last time I saw him, he was living with a sixteen-year-old runaway—he had just turned twenty-seven—and selling knock-off sunglasses and watches on the street.

That day I phoned him from Julian's he sounded stoned and surly, not at all pleased to hear me; he was doing the odd bit of construction work, he told me, to pay the rent, but his real job was managing indie rock bands, "the dudes who are making the real shit now, only the plastic capitalists can't deal with it." He had just lined up a booking at a club in Cincinnati. "Maybe I'll get a gig over there, for one of my bands, and come visit you."

"That'd be great," I said, and he gave a snorting laugh, either because he knew it wouldn't happen or because I so clearly didn't mean it. For a minute we were both silent, and then I reminded him to phone our mother, and he said he would, groaning, before telling me he had to go, he was supposed to check in on a rehearsal across town.

Upstairs, in the bedroom, the television was on, which meant Julian was settled in for the night. I grabbed the bottle of Glenfiddich from the bottom of the pewter hutch and locked myself in the study.

Pretty soon, swigging from the bottle, I was laughing and crying hysterically; one minute the scene with Sasha struck me as a great piece of comedy, I couldn't stop giggling, and a minute later I'd be convulsed with sobs, though in the schizzy way of drunkenness the sounds I was making seemed to come from somewhere outside me. Finally I fell into a gummy sleep, a long confused dream about searching for my brother in Citicorp Center, dodging the security guards as I darted through doors that said KEEP OUT. When I woke in the morning, with a woolly head and a foul taste in my mouth, I lay there for a long time, willing myself to do what was necessary: wash my face, pack my things, call for a minicab. Only what address could I give the driver? The hotel in Bloomsbury, the airport? And what would I do with myself then?

After what seemed like hours, when I knew the house must be empty, I forced myself, wincing, to stand up. A postcard of the Matterhorn lay on the carpet just inside the door. I turned it over. "Sorry," it said on the back. "I know I was a beast. It's my ghastly family, we must stay away from them in future." Underneath was a clumsy drawing of a creature with fangs.

Stupidly, stupidly, my heart gave a little leap. I sat back down, reading the message over and over, reading into it a whole slew of strangled feelings, love and regret and sorrow he didn't know how to express. But maybe he would learn, maybe everything would be different. And if I stayed there I could tell myself, I could even believe, that it wasn't from cowardice, it was out of magnanimity, womanly forgiveness. That night, when he returned from work, he was especially charming, he'd even brought me a bunch of white lilies, and before too long we wound up in bed.

Five

After that vaguely promising new start, the relationship went rapidly downhill, as any sensible person could have foreseen.

With the coming of summer, we became social animals, or rather he did, and I tagged along. There were dinners out with his colleagues, parties in Wimbledon and Richmond, a wedding reception at the Chelsea Arts Club. I bought a flowered tulle dress with sheer sleeves out of my dwindling funds, and smiled a lot, and deployed the word "lovely" with reckless abandon. In Richmond, our hostess apologized to me for the state of her garden, which was lush and gorgeous, all fragrant golds and purples and pale cream. "It's a positive jungle, isn't it? One of these days I swear I'll have the whole revolting mess dug up and tiled over." In Wimbledon, the colleague's wife apologized for the behavior of her "infant thugs," twin three-year-olds who were models of sweet decorum. As we listened to the toasts at the wedding reception, I was wondering if, when the bride's turn came, she would apologize for her choice of husband.

One Sunday in July, we were invited to lunch at his boss's house in Hampstead Garden Suburb. Lounging in a recliner on the lawn, Scotch in hand, Julian entertained the company with tales of his sojourn in Africa—the English tourists' preposterous mishaps, the feuds of his friend's Colonel Blimp father, the crocodile he had failed to kill. He was so genially, expansively male that he made the other men there seem like eunuchs.

Quite a lot of drinking went on that afternoon, before and during and after luncheon. When we got home, having yanked off his tie and loosened his shirt buttons, he poured himself a large tumbler of whiskey and seated himself in the blue armchair in the living room, his legs spread wide as he kept up a running commentary on the other guests. "Poor Reg, he's a good old sausage, but I sometimes wonder if his wife ever feeds him. I swear he was ogling the leftover gravy on my plate, I almost offered to let him lick it." But after a few minutes he fell abruptly silent. He got up with a purposeful air and poured himself more Scotch, he stared moodily into the glass before taking another gulp. When he raised his eyes to me, they were cold with loathing. "I hope you realize what a fool you made of yourself back there." His words weren't slurred at all, they were bitten off like ice chips. "Wittering on about that Kiwi." Then he stalked out, slamming the door.

It was so bizarre that for a minute I forgot to be mad. I just sat there like an idiot, waiting for him to come back and say he'd been a beast, at which point I could stalk out myself. Maybe, as I left, I would point out in a haughty voice that in fact it was Arthur, one of the colleagues, who had wittered on about "that Kiwi"—Katherine Mansfield—more than I had, evidently anxious to show that he wasn't just a policy nerd; he had read English at Oxford, he was an aesthete at heart. It had struck me that all of his coworkers except the boss seemed to cling to some other identity apart from the job. "Telling all those stories about Africa," I might say scathingly. "Honestly, how long have you been back? Four years, is it? It's pathetic."

Only he never descended the stairs to find me. For the second time, I spent the night on the couch in the study, the faint sound of his snores coming through the ceiling. For the second time, or was it the third, Eliot's voice was telling me to leave, phone a cab, get out of there at once, it didn't matter where. But I knew I wouldn't do it. I told myself it was what I deserved, what I had done to Eliot—tore him down to nothing, shouted every wounding thing I could think of. Then a crazy defiance flared in me: I was not to be gotten rid of so easily, I wasn't going to slink away, if that was what he wanted, I would stick it out until I'd said my piece. Rhetorical flourishes, phrases of great eloquence and concision, were forming in my mind for the final showdown.

Plus I had an article to finish. A month before, an old college friend, having heard about Eliot's death from Joannie, had written a letter of condolence and asked if I'd like to write for the literary journal he was editing at Bowling Green. "What about 2000 words on Katherine Mansfield? We're coming up to the hundredth anniversary of her birth." It was such a small thing, but it seemed huge at the time: to think the world had some use for me after all, my life wasn't a hundred percent pointless. (It was when Julian's boss had asked me how I was occupying myself in London that I had mentioned the article, and Arthur had launched into his commentary on "The Garden Party.") Already, having read the complete works, the letters, the journals, two biographies, I'd roughed out the piece, but it was still full of holes, and I'd promised to send it that week.

So the next morning, having waited for the sound of the front door closing, I got up and went resolutely to work. That evening, Julian sat at the kitchen table with the *Guardian* and started telling me, in a loathsomely chummy way, as though nothing had happened, about his day at the office, his and Pamela's meeting with the MP for Burnley. He explained why deregulating the City traders would have alarming consequences for financial stability. "They'd organized a protest outside the Houses of Parliament, but only eighteen people showed up. So much for our concerned citizenry."

Meanwhile I went on making a spaghetti bolognese in chilly silence—no matter what a shit he was being, I still felt duty-bound to provide supper, given that I was living there rent-free. I stirred and grated and sprinkled energetically, without once looking at him, though once we sat down to eat that became a little difficult. Still, I felt I had acquitted myself reasonably well, presenting myself not as an injured person, but as a stern and dignified one. After supper I returned to the study to pore over various befuddling articles on Gurdjieff, who'd either killed Mansfield with his punishing regimen or afforded her inner peace, depending on your point of view. Having brought down my nightgown and toilet things before he came back, as well as a blanket and pillow, I spent a perfectly comfortable night on the couch.

The next afternoon, while making myself a tuna sandwich, I switched on the kitchen radio to hear a woman with a piercing, Lady Bracknellish voice expostulating about the decline in the lapwing population since the introduction of chemical farming: "And have you read the latest Common Plant Survey?" No, the interviewer said meekly, she hadn't. "Far more useful to read that than to sit here chatting with me." It seemed that not only the corncrockle was vanishing, but the scarlet pimpernel and the campion and the lesser celandine too. "Soon the whole country will look like a golf course. You must know that marvelous Larkin poem: 'And that will be England gone.' So it will. Not just England, but the entire planet. Sooner than the ninnies in Westminster and Washington suppose."

"Can we get back to talking about your career?"

"I told you, I never thought of it as a career. I was simply curious about the way cells worked."

"You were pregnant when you had your first big breakthrough, weren't you?"

"Yes, with my oldest child. I took myself to a deserted island off the Welsh coast, my husband was positively livid."

"And you discovered the reason that a certain species of vole was particularly promiscuous."

"Absolutely insatiable. A single variation on a single chromosome, and they can't control their lust. Of course by the time I presented my first paper I was about to pop. Nobody took me seriously. They thought I was off my head."

"But then it was confirmed by other studies."

"Yes, by the academics. The men. So they saw there was something in it."

"Did you experience a lot of sexist bias when you were starting out?"

"I never bothered myself with that. I was too absorbed in what I was doing."

"And you didn't find any conflict between motherhood and your scientific work?"

"Not a bit of it. Anyway, I did most of my best science when the children were sleeping. Fortunately I never needed more than three or four hours a night, I was lucky that way."

"I remember seeing a charming photograph of one of your daughters playing with a mongoose you kept in your bedroom."

"Not a mongoose, I never had one of those. A ferret. Then there was Algernon, the python, he used to wrap himself round me when I slept. But the children weren't so fond of him. Or the rats, either."

"What are you working on now?"

"I'm having a frightful time with a butterfly enzyme that simply will not behave in the same way twice. But I think I could be on the trail of something useful. Something that might lead to a treatment for this beastly HIV."

The interviewer said they were running out of time, blah blah, thank you so much, most stimulating, and then, "We've been visiting with the distinguished geneticist Helena Denby, at her home in Devon. And now stay tuned for the final episode of *The Village Postmistress*, read by Scott Farnsworth, on *The Afternoon Play*."

"What an extraordinary idea. What she really means is 'Sasha, you worthless cunt.'" "My impossible mother... my diabolical mother." And once, "She fancies herself a scientist. She studies rats, very fitting."

The smart thing would be to keep my mouth shut, I knew that perfectly well. But I was still smarting about the Kiwi attack, hungering for revenge.

"I heard your mother on the radio today."

"Did you? And how was she?"

"Great. Fascinating, actually. What an amazing woman. Did you know she's working on a cure for AIDS?"

"As a matter of fact I didn't." He stood up abruptly, taking the paper with him.

But when we sat down to eat that night he said in a silky voice, "Tell me about Eliot," and then pressed me, with an air of sympathetic interest, for the sort of details he had never requested before: where had he grown up? where had I met him? what were his parents like? how did I get the news of his death? As I fumbled out my answers, he had the purposefully kindly air of a policeman coaxing information from a suspect. It made me more and more uneasy, but I didn't see the trap he was laying until it was too late.

"So," he said coolly, when I had cleared the table and served up the melon for dessert, "he might very well still be alive if you hadn't fucked him over."

"I didn't. I didn't fuck him over."

"Of course you did." His face was alight with triumph. "That must be why you're afraid to go back to America, everybody there blames you for his death. Is there going to be any coffee?"

I found myself shrieking the crude epithets of the hoodlums at Gurneyville High, those pasty, peaky-looking boys raised on a diet of starch and clearly marked out for a life of petty crime. "You're a real sick motherfucker, you know that?" I yelled, as I stormed up the stairs, and, leaning over the bannister, "You psycho bastard," before grabbing some clean underwear and a change of clothing and locking myself in the study for yet another night. The couch had begun to take on the indentations of my body, the spines of the books were making patterns in my dreams.

It seems incredible that I could stay there after that night, it makes my flesh crawl to remember it, but somehow I did, I clung on, telling myself he was the crazy one, when actually my terror of being on my own had grown so huge that anything, even Julian, even crying myself to sleep in the study, seemed less scary than any alternative I could think of. But things didn't stay as they were, they got a lot worse. He'd sit in the blue armchair, unmoving except for the hand carrying the glass or the cigarette to his mouth, explaining the ways I revolted him, a fantastic litany of small and large sins. I'd had parsnip puree smeared all over my chin when we went out for dinner with his university friends (though the wife of one of them had suggested we go together to the Tate that week, it was only because she felt sorry for me, I was so pathetic). My new black silk blouse looked like something a greengrocer's wife in Balham would wear to a funeral. My Katherine Mansfield piece sounded like some sozzled old poofta gassing on about beeooty. I was disgusting, I disgusted him, why didn't I at least blow my nose.

Sometimes I'd be the one seated, with him looming over me, the violence boiling in him, I could feel it, ready to explode. "Keep your hands off me," I'd yell, and he'd laugh and say he hadn't touched me. Then he'd brush his hand lightly, experimentally, across my throat, as though testing it, deciding whether to take both hands and squeeze until I stopped breathing. He liked that I was afraid, I could tell. He raised his hand to my face—trembling a little, the way it always did when he was angry—and made as though to slap me, before turning away abruptly and leaving the room. Another time he did hit me, a sharp slap on the cheek meant to humiliate more than hurt. I clenched my teeth and waited as he stood over me, swaying, grinning; it was like a game of who'd blink first. When he moved away, I stood and headed for the door, and he caught me by the arm and twisted it hard behind my back, still grinning. Does that count as domestic violence? There were never any bruises, he never even kicked in a door. In fact I was more violent than he was; once I picked up a knife from the kitchen counter and brandished it hysterically, but he managed to wrest it away from me without much trouble.

If I looked at myself in the mirror in the mornings, my face seemed to dissolve, like a character's in a cheap sci-fi flick. Most shameful of all, I found myself whispering, "I love you," the words slipping out without my volition, though never, thank God, when he was present. I couldn't understand it, I didn't believe it for a minute, but when I woke in the study at three in the morning, groggy with sleep, or heard the front door shut behind him as he left for work, there were those words again, before I could stop them.

Meanwhile I kept writing my lying letters—to my mother, to Joannie, to Eliot's parents in St. Cloud. Feeling sick to my stomach, I responded to my mother-in-law's outpourings with pages and pages of phony memories, stirring accounts of incidents from my marriage that had never happened, or happened so long ago I'd forgotten the details. My whole life now seemed like such a betrayal of Eliot, a few more falsehoods couldn't possibly matter. To Joannie I admitted that I was not just a tourist any longer, I was living with an Englishman in London, not that I'd forgotten Eliot, or ever would. She was glad for me, she answered, enclosing photos of her new baby daughter in little ruffled bonnets: "I never knew it was possible to love another human being like this. It's like falling in love *every day*."

I told no one the truth of what was happening—not Joannie, not my mother, not the friend's wife, who phoned after all, and off we went to see the Turners. It felt like a perversion, a kinky sexual secret, he had tapped into some hidden, degraded part of me that could never be shared with anyone else. And so I dissembled, I went on calling things lovely and burbling to my mother about Big Ben. I gave nothing away until the Wednesday afternoon, three months and two days after I'd finally moved out, when I bumped into Isabel, literally, in the vast domed Reading Room in the British Museum, and burst into tears, and it all came tumbling out.

Six

It was when she said, "I was sorry to hear about you and Julian," that the tears started gushing. We had both bent down to pick up the books I'd knocked to the floor when I'd jostled against her; while we were still upright I had said Sorry sorry so sorry, she had asked me how I was and I had cried out manically that I was fine, just fine, couldn't be better, how was she; then I went into a squat to retrieve the books, and she knelt also, our heads almost touching. That's when she said it.

A pair of legs in baggy trousers stopped beside me. "Are you all right?" I looked up, sniffling, at a woman with a bowl haircut and bulging eyes. "She's fine," Isabel said firmly, "she's just tired." "Are you sure?" the woman asked, and Isabel said, "Quite sure, thank you." "Go home and get some sleep then," the woman said brusquely, and walked off.

I rose to my feet. "She's right," I said, trying to laugh. "I really do need to sleep." I wiped my eyes. "Or maybe a drink." In my bedsit in Camden Town I was drinking cheaper whiskey than I had at Julian's.

"Shall we go to a pub?" Isabel the Good, Sasha had called her. If I hadn't been so lonely I would have said no thanks; I might have said, Please don't suppose I require your benevolence. But the truth was, I did require it; I badly needed to listen to someone else's voice for a change, instead of the one in my head.

So I said sure, with an ungracious shrug, and she went to leave the books in her carrel while I fetched my coat and bag.

At first we made civilized conversation. I asked her what she was working on in the Reading Room: something about the ancient Greeks again, and the evolution of tragedy. When she asked me the same question, I told her a lie. I was actually there to research the history of Toby jugs for a glossy American magazine—I'd been managing to scrape a living by writing about cigarette picture cards, Regency snuffboxes, all manner of things about which I knew nothing and cared even less. My wobbly desk in Camden Town was littered with used phone cards for five-p-a-minute long distance calls; I conducted my business with editors from the pay phone in the front hall. But for Isabel I wanted to sound intellectually respectable. So I said I'd been working up an essay on literary insomniacs: how maybe the alterations of mind that came with sleeplessness—all those feverish galloping thoughts, those stark revelations at four a.m. (I was in that state myself when the idea of such a piece had occurred to me a few nights before)—could feed into the work.

Oh, yes, she said, in fact there were South American tribes that stayed awake for days before performing their holy dances, to attain the requisite ecstatic state. "Or the women do. The men just take peyote."

On we went, talking about highfalutin topics like creation myths—the Hindus believed the world was born through God dancing, she told me, the pagans that dance had roused the dead planet earth into life—until I was well into my second Bell's, when my veneer cracked. First I let out a hiccup, and then I was crying again. "Oh, God, I'm sorry," I said. "It's just that . . . I really haven't been sleeping. I can't seem to sleep."

She looked so distressed that it made me cry harder. "What was wrong with the pewter hutch that night?" I asked, sobbing. A total non sequitur.

"What?"

"The night you came to supper. You kept looking at the stuff on the pewter hutch, as though it was upsetting you somehow."

"Oh . . . the Welsh dresser."

"Whatever. Why did it bother you like that? Was it the bee?"

She ducked her head; she started rearranging the salt and pepper shakers on the scarred table top.

"Tell me," I demanded, curiosity drying my tears.

It was because she'd seen it happen before, she said cautiously. "With the others. They'd move in with their grandmother's Spode teacups, or their collection of glass animals, and then a month later they'd have gone, and the next time I went, somebody else's Wedgewood would be there, or a silver candelabra."

"But why? Why did they go?" Julian had only ever mentioned his old girlfriends in passing, and always in eye-rolling ironic mode: Deirdre, who'd been tiresomely whiney; Claire, an ex-tennis champion turned political activist turned some sort of functionary for the SDP-Liberal alliance, who later became a lesbian and decamped to live with her former editor from *Spare Rib*. I'd found the name Rowena in various books in his house: she'd been an actress, he'd said, but more offstage than on: "a drama queen, I couldn't take the constant hysterics after a while."

"Probably for the same reason you did," she said. "Or that I suppose you did. I don't imagine he was terribly pleasant to any of them after a while." She hesitated. "I know Rowena swallowed a bottle of pills and had to have her stomach pumped."

"Oh my God. And here I thought it was just me." It was true: he'd convinced me that his contempt was reserved for me, for my accent and my general inappropriateness and what I'd done to Eliot; it had never occurred to me that anyone else had aroused the same loathing.

"No. But I'd thought that because you were American you'd be a bit tougher somehow. More well-armored. Then I saw that you weren't really. So the rearrangement of the Welsh dresser...it seemed a bad sign." (But then they're all a bit pathetic, aren't they, Junes, Sasha had said.)

"I wish you'd warned me."

"Sent you an anonymous letter? 'Flee, fair damsel, you too will be destroyed'? But he'd have known where it came from, and you'd have felt sorry for him, thinking he had two mad sisters instead of one."

"Was he always that way? Even when he was little?"

"He wasn't one of those boys who tear the wings off flies, if that's what you mean. At least not that I know of. But he was horrid to the gardener's children at Sidworth, he bullied them terribly, and went into fearsome rages if he didn't get his way. Not a very *nice* child. Though it took me ages to admit it. He'd been my adored baby brother, you see, I used to plead with Nanny to let me help her bathe him. I don't know when I started to be a bit frightened of him. But it was a relief when he went off to prep school."

"How old was he?"

"Seven."

"Jesus."

"It was considered quite usual back then," she said dryly. "Still is, I believe. Though it's true he used to write to Mother begging her to take him away. But she said all boys hated their prep schools at first, he'd soon come to love it like everyone else."

We sat in silence for a minute. "It's strange," I said then. "Knowing about the others—knowing he was the same with them—I'm not sure if I feel better or worse. It's as though it wasn't even special to me, all those things I've been going over and over in my head. Of course I should have known, it's blindingly obvious now I think about it, of course it wouldn't have been just me. But it's kind of deflating in some weird way. I guess even masochists want to think they're special. It's crazy, isn't it." Worst of all, though I didn't say so, was thinking I might have been supplanted already, some other woman was crying and raging in the house on Rona Road even as we sat there. He could have forgotten all about me, while I had been thinking of nothing but him.

"Not really. We probably all want to think our suffering is unique."

"I'm not sure it's even worthy to be called suffering. Probably it's just my pride that's hurt, not my heart. My deep heart's core. I'm not starving, and I'm not riddled with cancer, and . . . suffering is when someone dies. Like your husband in Greece. Your lover." She gave a start. "Sorry, I shouldn't have said that."

"It's all right. It was a long time ago. And even that sort of suffering isn't unique. It happens all the time, you read it in the papers every day, you see those women in Lebanon wailing over their husbands' bodies. Or their children's. Or their brothers'. Someone once said that was the great mystery, that the world is so beautiful, and yet so full of torment. Another thing that's blindingly obvious, maybe. But I think about it quite often. Oh dear. This isn't a very cheerful conversation, is it."

I wanted to tell her everything then: about Eliot, and my father, and the Irishwoman who lived downstairs from me in Camden Town, how sometimes at night I could hear her, through the cracks in the floorboards, cursing and sobbing. And wondering how long she had been like that, if maybe both of us would stay there forever, consumed with rage for some man who had long since forgotten what we looked like.

Instead, I said, "I want to read your book," and she laughed.

"Please don't. It will bore you terribly, and you'll wish you hadn't, and next time we see each other you won't know what to say." I was warmed by her saying that, by the assumption that we'd see each other again. Did she come to the Reading Room very often? I asked, and she said every Wednesday, she had to finish another book to satisfy her department at Kings. "But the truth is, I've lost interest in my subject. I'm thinking of writing something else entirely, maybe something on those creation myths we were talking about."

"Then I'll read that one," I said. "When it's finished."

"You may have to wait a long time. But are you planning to stay here? You aren't moving back to America?"

"Oh, no," I said, shocked. "I love it here." She gave me a startled look, and I realized how ridiculous that sounded, after my litany of woe. Suddenly I started to laugh, and a moment later she did too, not demurely, politely, but in merry peals that made her face go pink. We were like two giddy schoolgirls— airborne, floating free.

I slept much better that night. And when I woke I remembered that the world was beautiful and full of torment, which seemed like a thought to hang onto.

The next Wednesday I made sure to be in the Reading Room—I had an assignment to write about Gallé lamps—and roamed around shamelessly, checking out all the carrels, until I spotted her. We went to lunch in the museum cafeteria, and again the next Wednesday, and the next. Over the following weeks I did tell her about Eliot, and my father, and the trip to Devon, and even the Irishwoman, but she told me things too, though never unless I asked her. "Do all Americans ask so many questions?" she asked me once, sounding puzzled.

"Only when we're trying to get to know someone. Does that seem strange to you? Or vulgar? Like some Wild West roughneck invading your privacy?"

"Actually," she said, "I think I rather like it."

It was easy to get her to talk about Lucy, with a pride imperfectly masked by irony: "The offspring," she called her, when she told me how brilliantly she was doing at French, or how she had volunteered to tutor children from the local primary school. "She's becoming terribly judgmental about me, I suppose that was inevitable, she doesn't think what I do has much use in the world. It's her father she admires, and of course that's right, he did do something to change the world, or at least try, though if he were around she'd probably find things to judge him for too."

"And do you wish he were?"

"Not so intensely now. Not in the old way. But for Lucy, yes. And that time in Greece cast a very long shadow. I don't do enough, I know that. Just sign petitions, send some money to refugee charities. It isn't much. But I'm supervising a student now who had to flee Beirut after her father spoke out against the government. They came and took him away, they can't find out where he is. Once I would have said, Oh, how dreadful, I would have pitied her, but I might have felt embarrassed too when I was around her. Now it doesn't seem so unimaginable, it's not like something that happened on another planet. Whatever good that might do her."

"Have you ever told her about Stavros?"

"I don't think that would be appropriate. But I'm almost sure she senses something. At least she tells me more than she tells anyone else at the college. And lets me give her money for food. She's very proud, she used to come to class half starved rather than ask."

Another time I asked her if she'd ever been in love with anyone since he died.

No, she said, not even close. "I suppose that sounds terribly Victorian, but it's not a deliberate thing. I didn't swear to be faithful to him unto death. I just haven't met anyone else who mattered to me in the same way. Not that I've been . . . I've had the odd relationship over the years." Only the year before, it seemed, she'd had an affair with an art history professor from the Courtauld: he'd been a bit pompous, she said, but she'd managed to ignore that until the time they went with Sasha to the National Gallery, where, in front of the Wilton Diptych, he expounded at length on the possible Italian, French, and Rhenish influences, and the stylistic similarities to the Beaufort Book of Hours. "And finally Sasha said, 'You talk about art like a policeman trying to solve a crime. Like the murderer's in hiding but you've figured out where to find him.' Of course he was outraged, he couldn't stop talking about it afterward, wanting me to apologize over and over, but actually I could see her point. Things were never the same between us after that."

I knew she went to see Sasha every week; she would mention a film they'd seen together, or an exhibition they'd gone to. But once, after Sasha had been "difficult," she said mournfully, "She really was special when she was young, you know—the golden girl." And she told me how, at eight, Sasha would read abstruse commentaries on mathematics under the covers at night, how she'd announced she was going to prove Fermat's last theorem when she grew up; then how she'd come back from school in a fury, aged six, because the teacher had said she had to be an angel in the Christmas pageant, when she'd had her heart set on being the donkey. "And really, she did look like an angel. With all those blond curls, and cornflower-blue eyes. No wonder everybody spoiled her."

"But you must have been beautiful too," I said, and she shook her head.

"Oh, no, I was horribly podgy and plain. Utterly charmless, as Mother used to say. Sometimes even within my hearing."

"I don't believe that." But the next time we met, she produced an old snapshot from her bag, a tiny black-and-white photo with scalloped edges: there she was, plain and podgy, just as she'd said, slumped on a bench, her head drooping. "My God," I said. "You do look pathetic."

"I told you."

"How old were you when this was taken?" I turned it over, and read the date on the back: 21 May 1960.

"It was my twelfth birthday. My father took it, he'd come from London for the occasion."

"You don't look like a birthday girl at all. More as though somebody has just died."

"Somebody had," she said, and her voice was dry in the way of dry ice; her face told me the subject was closed, I wasn't to trespass on this any further. She took the photo from me, replacing it in her bag and clicking it shut. No entry. As for the question of who had died: it would be months before I learned the answer to that one.

Part Two

Seven

Her name was Madeleine, and she'd come to live with them at Sidworth when Isabel was nine. She wasn't like Helena's other friends, the ones who arrived for the weekend house parties and laughed delightedly as they asked Isabel trick questions: had she ever seen a naked man, did her mother tell her all her secrets, what was her father up to these days. Maddy never did that, and her voice was different from theirs, slower, with a faint accent. Her clothes weren't as elaborate, or her hair either, which was drawn into a bun at the nape of her neck. "Positively nunlike," one of the house-guests said, though she reminded Isabel of the drawing of Jane in her copy of *Jane Eyre*. And she had a slight limp—apparently there had been some unpleasantness in Germany, that was the only explanation ever given. But everyone agreed that she was terribly clever, just as clever as Helena. "Oh, much cleverer than I am," Helena said airily, sounding pleased.

What mattered most to Isabel at first was that Maddy woke up early. Helena never stirred until ten or so, and then she breakfasted from a tray in her room, so Mrs. Spargo, the housekeeper, didn't bother to light the kitchen Aga until nine. With Julian at boarding school, Isabel was on her own every morning, making tea and porridge for herself on the Baby Belling in the freezing kitchen, before leaving for school. That all changed once Maddy arrived: Maddy would be sitting at the table when she came down, with the kettle boiling and the porridge waiting for her.

After a few weeks she somehow found herself telling Maddy things she'd never talked about before, like how scary it would be if people thought you were dead and you woke in the ground with your mouth full of earth; you could scream and scream, and nobody would hear you. Or how, though her mother had scoffed at the superstitious nonsense taught in her Religious Studies class, she sometimes prayed.

"What do you pray for?" Maddy asked.

To be good, she said. "Because sometimes I'm afraid I could be evil and not know it."

"I see. And why do you want to be good? To go to heaven?"

Of course not, she said. She didn't believe in heaven.

"Well, that's all right then. As long as you aren't doing it to get into heaven. Because then it wouldn't really be about being good, would it? Anyway, if you were really evil I suspect you wouldn't worry about it. Now get over here, your hair looks a sight this morning." Isabel went and stood between her knees as she untangled it and redid the plaits. It wasn't very hygienic to be messing with hair in the kitchen, Maddy said, but then it wasn't hygienic to let the dogs sleep in there either. "I daresay your hair is no more infested than theirs is."

"At least I don't roll in manure."

"Which is very admirable of you."

And Isabel felt they were being terribly witty.

It bothered her that the weekend guests, especially the women, sometimes talked about Maddy as though she were a joke. ("Of course Isabel adores Madeleine," she heard one of them say. "She follows her around like a little dog.") "Be a dear, Maddy, and fetch me my glasses from the conservatory, won't you?" This from a rackety countess who was always complaining about her servants going Bolshie ("They'll murder me in my bed one day, just wait, you'll read about it in the papers"). An aging actress who'd been one of Isabel's particular tormentors ("And what would you say about that man over there? Would you say he's drunk, or just naturally vile?") called Maddy "darling Madeleine," in a sneery voice. "I'm sure you're a great help to Helena with her researches; you're so terribly learned, aren't you. At least that's what we hear." Isabel longed for Maddy to rebuff them, to wither them with a look or a scathing retort. But Maddy, for all her famous cleverness, never did. Alone with Isabel, she was wise and merry, she could make even electromagnetism sound interesting, and tell gripping stories about pagan gods and goddesses, but around those women she receded into blankness, her eyes grew opaque.

So it was Isabel who took revenge, though not to the women's faces—that would only have incurred her mother's wrath. But in the kitchen on Monday mornings, she'd put on a show for Maddy, fluttering her eyes like the actress or raising one eyebrow like the countess, mimicking their separate drawls: "One does everything for them, everything, and where is their loyalty? Where is their gratitude?" Mindful of her duty, Maddy would tell her sternly not to be disrespectful, but a minute later she'd burst out laughing: "It's very naughty of me, but . . . goodness, they really are gorgons, aren't they?"

But the second winter that Maddy was at Sidworth there were no more stories of Greek gods, and Maddy stopped laughing altogether. She no longer teased Isabel, or kissed her when she got all her French verbs right; she didn't seem to notice if Isabel's braids were straggly. Her voice was flat and toneless, sometimes she didn't even answer when Isabel spoke to her, as though she hadn't heard. It was as unrewarding as talking to Helena, who had a habit of tapping her foot or drumming her fingers on the arm of her chair the whole time, to hurry Isabel along.

Actually Helena could be just as impatient with Maddy, except on certain occasions when she'd joined them for breakfast; she seemed softer, almost girlish on those mornings, keeping her eyes on Maddy as Maddy attended to household matters—creating seating plans for the dinner on Saturday evening or making small changes, in her neat hand, on the menu

Mrs. Spargo had presented for her inspection. That winter, though, her mother never came down for breakfast; day after day, it was just the two of them, Maddy and Isabel, sitting in near-silence until Mark, who served as chauffeur as well as gardener, brought the Daimler round to take her to school.

For two years, she'd been sure of Maddy's full attention, she'd expanded within it; now she tried different stratagems to get it back. She twirled around the kitchen showing off her steps from ballet class, she bought Maddy little presents with her pocket money—a paisley square, a facsimile of a Victorian flower book. She attempted cynical, grown-up talk, parroting remarks she'd overheard from her mother's guests: "Isn't it a pity that Mr. Stillwell's nose turns so red when he drinks?" "I do hope the buggers at Cheam won't prey on Julian...such a pretty boy." She tried the opposite tactic, acting the brat, she'd play scales with her fork on her empty juice glass or chant nonsense rhymes in mangled French. None of it worked. Sometimes the kitchen was empty when she came downstairs; she was back to making her own tea, scraping bits of burnt porridge off the cooker.

Then it was spring, God was in his heaven: day after day the sun shone in a cloudless sky, the apple trees in the orchard were covered in pink blossom, newborn lambs frolicked on the hill opposite. On the third Saturday in May Isabel was invited to a class-mate's birthday party in Ashburton. Months earlier, Maddy had ordered her a new dress from London, white organza with a blue silk sash that Isabel was tying into a bow when Maddy appeared in her room for the first time in weeks. She hitched the bow up a notch, she patted Isabel on the head, talking all the while in a false glittery voice.

"She kept exclaiming over the sash, it was the blue of the Aegean, she said, I must see the Aegean one day, I must promise her, only it didn't feel like she was talking to me at all, she was just *talking*, running on and on. She began steering me downstairs, almost pushing me, with her hand on my back, to where Mark was waiting to drive me to the party. Gabbling about how I must take my mac and my brolly, because the weather people had predicted a storm, though what did any of them know, she said, it was a glorious day, simply glorious, with a throb of rapture to her voice. Then she turned and went back upstairs."

Later Isabel could hardly remember the party, except for the birthday girl's mother, who was probably the reason she'd been invited. She and Alison Lockwood weren't friendly at school, but whenever Mrs. Lockwood saw Isabel in the village, or at school concerts, she always pounced on her with questions. The licentious house parties at Sidworth, the disgusting experiments on vermin: all these were subjects of gossip in the Teign Valley. There was also speculation about the banishment of Isabel's father, years earlier, to a flat Helena owned in London.

"I heard your mother on the wireless a few weeks ago," Mrs. Lockwood said, "all about genes, and how everything we do is really down to cells," while Alison squealed with delight over a pair of brightly striped socks someone had given her. "Of course she's so terribly brainy, I couldn't follow half of what she was saying. What a clever woman! Are you as brainy as your mother?" There seemed to be no good answer to that, and Isabel was too preoccupied to think of one. She kept remembering Maddy's voice, but she wasn't sure what she had said herself, if there was something she should have said and hadn't. She needed to talk to Maddy some more, she had to ask her why she'd sounded like that.

And then Mark was late picking her up. The cake had been cut and eaten, the mothers, or au pair girls with exotic accents, had all come to fetch the others. Mrs. Lockwood carried off the smeared plates, and Isabel was left alone in the sitting room with Alison, who told her about the super mill house in the Dordogne they'd be renting again that summer. She was describing the rides at the village fete when the bell rang, and Isabel heard Mark whispering to Mrs. Lockwood in the doorway. A moment later Mrs. Lockwood came into the room and asked if Isabel would like to stay the night: "Wouldn't it be nice for you and Alison to spend a little time together? I mean proper time, to get to know each other better." A look of horror passed over Alison's face.

She wanted to go home, Isabel said loudly, louder than she'd meant to.

"I really think it might be better, dear, if you stayed with us," Mrs. Lockwood said, with deliberate gentleness. Then she knew for sure that something terrible had happened, and hurled herself at Mark, who had edged into the room, clutching him around the waist like a four-year-old. "Please," she said, "please take me home."

When she was little she'd always begged to sit next to him in the front; now, having led her outside in silence, he opened the front door, and she slid inside. Several times on the drive back, he cleared his throat, about to speak, but he never did, and she was too frightened to ask. The sky was a hard bright blue; the wind was perfectly still. Maddy had been right about the forecast.

Back at Sidworth, Alice, the secretary Helena had hired a few weeks before, sat her down and broke the news; her mother was much too upset to see anyone, Alice said. "You can imagine what a dreadful shock this has been for her," she went on, as though everyone's first sympathy must be for Helena—as though, even, it was a little inconsiderate of Maddy to kill herself at Sidworth, where Helena, as she liked to remind people, had lived her whole life. "But of course she was disturbed in her mind." Later Alice came to Isabel's bedroom with a cameo brooch Maddy used to wear pinned to her collar. "Your mother wanted you to have it," Alice said. "She gave it to Madeleine herself, a special present," emphasizing the last two words, watching Isabel avidly, as though wanting to say more.

It was Sasha who filled in the gory details; she'd overheard one of the maids telling Nanny how Maddy had hanged herself in the greenhouse where the orchids were grown. Helena had found her dangling from a hook. "Wasn't it lucky," Sasha said "well, not lucky exactly, but you know what I mean, the whole thing could have come crashing down, because really, when you think about it, a person must weigh a lot more than a pot, even a little thin person like Maddy." She was heady with the drama of it all, being starved for excitement: nursery life had begun to pall for her by then. But a few days later Helena sacked Nanny for talking about it within Sasha's hearing.

"So Sasha too lost her great love that week."

"Do you know why she did it?" I asked.

"Why?" she repeated, fierce suddenly. "Because my mother, who was her lover, was finished with her, she wanted her out. Of course I didn't know that then. I thought of her as mine, belonging to me, I thought she was happy just sitting at breakfast with me making little jokes. But then I never saw her as a separate person, I never asked her anything about her life. Like what the unpleasantness was in Germany. Maybe she was Jewish, I don't even know that much."

(She didn't say, "She was like a second mother to me." She said, "She was the person I thought of as my mother.")

It was eight years before she learned the truth, and then it was from the countess she used to imitate for Maddy all those years before (it turned out her butler really had been a revolutionary, smuggling explosives for the IRA). They were sitting on the terrace at

Sidworth before lunch, drinking gin, when the other woman said idly, "Of course you must have realized that Madeleine was your mother's lover." No, Isabel said, she hadn't realized. The countess's eyebrows rose.

"It's not as though Helena made any secret of it at the time; everybody knew she'd washed her hands of men, and really, who could blame her? It was just a shame that Madeleine took it so badly when she finished it. But of course she loved your mother desperately, poor thing, and quite apart from that, there was the problem of where she could go. She couldn't very well return to teaching school, but nor could Helena let her stay here, you can see that, it would have been too awkward for everyone. Out of the question, really."

Isabel went on sipping her gin. At luncheon she sat between a man who talked to her about Harold Wilson's relations with the trade unions and one who told her about the molecular hybridization of radioactive DNA. She kissed her mother good-bye as always before Mark's successor drove her to the train. "And all the while," she told me, with a jerky laugh, "I kept thinking, I got it all wrong, it was never me Maddy loved best."

Back in Cambridge that night, she dreamed she was in the rose garden at Sidworth, she could see Maddy at her bedroom window, but though she kept calling to her, shouting out her name, Maddy never once looked down. Finally she ran into the house, up the stairs, but there was only a long white corridor that stretched on and on, like the dream itself. She kept trying to escape, to wake herself up, when suddenly the figure from the window came walking toward her. Except it wasn't Maddy at all, it was her mother, dressed like Alice in Wonderland, in a white eyelet dress with a blue satin sash, and long blond curls framing her wrinkled face.

"Only of course it wasn't an Alice in Wonderland dress, it was mine. The dress that I'd worn on the day of Alison Lockwood's party."

Eight

M y father's desertion had left chaos behind, our
misery compounded by the intrusions of strangers. Suddenly there were all these new people in our
lives, like Miss Rader, the county welfare worker, with
her buckteeth and her clipboard, and Mr. Coleman,
her supervisor, who sometimes drove my mother to
the office in Canton to fill out forms but just as often
brought them to the house and questioned her in the
living room: was anybody else contributing to the family finances—any relation, lodger, boyfriend she had
not declared? Was she the expected beneficiary of any
will or trust, had she at any time traded food stamps
for alcohol, tobacco, or proscribed substances? What
was her job history, how would she describe her mar-
ketable skills? What had she done with the Medicaid
forms they'd sent her? Once, for no reason I could
think of, Miss Rader yanked up my T-shirt to show
Mr. Coleman how skinny I was; for weeks afterward I
burned with shame at the memory.

Then the Methodists started coming around, with
their casseroles of beans, or franks and beans, brown
food in ugly brown Crock-Pots, but it gave them the

right to ask my mother if there'd been trouble with other women, if my father had ever "messed around" with young girls. Meanwhile Adam was hiding behind the door in his underpants, listening in. I waited for my mother to tell those women to mind their own business, and anyway we were Catholics—my father's religion—but she just looked around helplessly, as though searching for answers in the dustballs on the carpet. "Not so's far as I know," was all she said.

"He never did that, I know he didn't," I hissed to Adam, but his perfect trust in me had vanished along with our father, he didn't believe in my omniscience anymore. My assurances that wherever Daddy was he would never stop loving us no longer sounded convincing even to me.

Mrs. Roy hoped to reclaim my mother for Protestantism. Adam and I were made to go to Bible class and sing "Jesus is my sunshine" with runny-nosed kids half our age. Mrs. Kinney was always squatting down to peer into our faces, her breath smelling of Luden's cherry cough drops. Jesus wanted me for a sunbeam, she said, and was I doing enough to help poor Mommy with the housework? They said Adam was the man of the house now; they told him Mr. Eberhard, their pastor, had been the sole support of his widowed mother from the age of nine, rising at dawn to go from house to house lighting people's boilers.

Instead of going home after school, I started haunting the squat concrete library on Main Street, where at least I'd be left alone. Under the indifferent gaze of the librarian, I'd head for the back section, where the grown-up books were, looking for kindly faces or pretty pictures on the jackets. That's how I stumbled on the novels of Miss Read, their covers showing the hedgerows and damson trees and duck ponds my father used to conjure up. In that pastoral English idyll good always prevailed, and even the poor were devoid of malice. There were no sixteen-year-old boys driving around in pickup trucks looking for skunks or rabbits or even dogs to shoot. None of the women told stories of their husbands' filthy sexual habits, or talked about the jigaboos and the crooked Jew lawyers down in the city. A comforting benevolence prevailed. That, I thought, was how it was in England.

A while later I graduated to *Jane Eyre* and *Pride and Prejudice* and the novels of Trollope, who filled up a whole metal shelf toward the back of the building. And past Leon Uris, just before you got to the Woodworking and Home Repairs section, was *Brideshead Revisited*, which seemed to me more tragic and exalted than anything. I had never heard of Anglophilia, I thought my worshipful fervor was unique to me, every banal revelation I came to was mine alone.

Of course Sidworth wasn't Pemberley, it wasn't Brideshead—there were no gazebos, no swans or private chapels, not even a long sweep of drive; it was not a castle but a large pale Jacobean manor house, with curved gables jutting upward from the roof—but still it was closer than anything I'd ever seen. I couldn't look at Isabel directly, I heard myself talking to her in a falsely breezy voice, as though to show I wasn't overawed . . . as though I was used to ancient-looking studded doors and mullioned windows, to paneled entry halls with vast fireplaces and carved oak staircases twisting upward. In fact it wasn't thrilling to be there, to see her in that setting, but weirdly painful; I felt too agitated to take it in properly. Certainly it didn't help that Helena, when Isabel brought me to her study, turned her head a bare few inches, nodded at me once, and went back to dictating into a tape recorder. We backed out in silence: only when we were out on the terraced lawn, heading toward what Isabel called her "patch," did she refer to it. "I'm sorry she was so horrid, but she knows about Julian, you see. She thinks you might report back to him."

"It's okay . . . She reminds me of those pictures of Edith Sitwell."

The "patch" turned out to be an enclosed precinct within the grounds, five minutes' walk from the house; her mother had signed over to her what used to be the home of the gardener in her grandfather's time, a cottage and garden and small orchard contained within faded red brick walls. We stepped through an oval door into the orchard, its rows of twisted apple trees just coming into blossom, with clumps of lavender fanning out around their roots. Along the far wall, past the trees, were scattered clumps of pink lilies; to the right was a high iron gate, painted white, between two brick pillars topped by chipped stone lions.

She led me through the overgrown grass down the rows of trees, touching them lightly as she named each one: Laxton's Superb, Ribston Pippin: old varieties, she said, not disease-proof the way the newer strains were, but in the autumn she would pick the healthy fruit and make chutney and apple butter. She yanked, frowning, at the ivy that was growing up the nearest wall: "there's nothing so destructive to brick as ivy, but I can't seem to get it under control." Then, when we passed through the gate into her garden, she took me from rose to rose. Blush Noisette was wonderfully reliable, she told me, it bloomed and bloomed and never gave any trouble. Glory John was prone to brown spot, but its scent was her favorite. Altissimo was blowsy, a little vulgar, but she loved its scarlet color. Madame Alfred Carrière was very accommodating, requiring less sun than the others. "If you ever need a rose for a north wall, do keep her in mind."

Something violent flared in me then. Did she really not know there were people in the world who would never need a rose for a north wall, who might live in dreary bedsits forever, like Mr. Bleaney, and that I might be one of them? Was she so unaware that other people, most people, had to get through life without owning orchards, without the certainties that were her fucking birthright? For the past year, we'd been maintaining the polite fiction that we were equals; now I saw how false that was—and how conscious she must have been of its falseness, that was the worst part. All along she'd been humoring me.

"Thanks for the tip," I said, heavily sarcastic. "Madame Alfred Carrière. Great for a north wall. I'll make a note of it, I'm sure it'll come in handy any day now."

She stared at me, a tremor passed over her face. But all she said was, "Why don't you sit down. I'll go make the tea." So I sat at the weathered table in the corner of the garden, under a flowering tree, consciously inhaling the smell as though it were part of a yoga ritual: breath in, breath out, calm down. In a few minutes she emerged again, with a wooden tray bearing a small flowered teapot and two brown mugs. "Maddy gave me this teapot," she said, in a high brittle voice. "For my tenth birthday. Maddy was the woman I thought of as my real mother. She killed herself just before I turned twelve. Do you take sugar?"

Like Julian, her hands shook when she was angry; I had never had occasion to notice that before. For a second we bristled at each other, one step from outright rancor, but we stopped short.

"Okay," I said. "I get it. You didn't grow up in Paradise."

"Not exactly."

"It's just that this place looks more like the Garden of Eden than anything I've ever seen."

"And you know how that story ended."

"Maddy was the one who died just before they took that photo you showed me."

She nodded.

"But . . . but why?"

And so she told me. Later that night, when she'd opened the bottle of wine I'd brought, it was my turn to reminisce about my childhood. I wouldn't be there, I said—in England, in Devon, at Sidworth—if it hadn't been for my father. "So that's something. We should drink to him for that."

She was stirring tomatoes and basil and chicken breasts in a pot on the stove, the little radio next to the sink was playing Chopin nocturnes, when I asked, "What about your father? I asked Julian about him once, and he nearly bit my head off. But he took that picture of you, didn't he, on your birthday?"

"He's dead now," she said. "Oh, damn, I forgot the garlic." She went into the pantry and emerged with a few loose cloves.

"You never seem to talk about him."

"I didn't really see him much after he went to London. A few times a year."

"What about Julian? Did he see him?"

She frowned down at the cookbook. "Not very often. I don't think I have any stock cubes, I'll have to make do with water."

I went to sleep that night in Lucy's sky-blue room, in a high iron bed covered in a faded quilt, surrounded by David Bowie posters and paintings of dogs and horses. The next morning we made a circuit of woods and lake and a meadow full of poppies; there were swaths of purple foxgloves in the woods and water birds skimming the surface of the lake, creating ripples of light. When we got back to the cottage, the phone was ringing in the living room.

"I can't, Mother, that would be extremely rude...No, I can't. Tell him I'll see him next time...That's not a very nice thing to say. I'm sure he won't mind. I'm not the one he came to see, after all. But make my excuses, won't you, and give him my love."

"I gather that was your mother," I said, when she came into the kitchen.

"That's right. Who has just put the phone down on me."

"What was it you were refusing to do?"

"Come to dinner tonight. Alone—that was the sticking point. Because Roger's going to be there, he's coming over from Oxford just for the night."

"Who's Roger?"

"As a matter of fact," she said, with a grimace, "as a matter of fact he's Julian's father." She marched to the sink and filled the kettle, the noise of water rushing into metal making speech impossible. Her mouth was pursed into a thin line; I thought she might be regretting having told me, so I left her there and went into the garden. But soon she brought out a tray with Maddy's teapot and two mugs. As we sat among the roses, the wood pigeons moaning monotonously in the distance, I heard the next part of the story.

Helena claimed she'd meant to tell them all when they were old enough. It was Sasha going off the rails that forced her hand. Sasha, who had been her favorite—everyone's favorite—and was now causing havoc in the household, climbing out windows at night to meet the local yobbos at the bottom of the drive, bringing them back to the house when everyone was asleep. In the morning there were sticky puddles of beer on the sitting room carpet, and a sweet heavy smell hung in the air. Small items went missing—a silver cigarette case, an Art Deco paper knife. Helena was ready to phone the police, but Sasha insisted she'd taken them herself: "I had to raise some money, din't I, to help Sally out; her mum's thrown her out the house and she had no money to doss down anywhere." She had adopted the vernacular of her new friends, and their reproachful whine. Helena threatened her with boarding schools in Scotland, but she wouldn't be cowed. "Go on then. I could run away easier from there than here, counnit I?"

Isabel was studying for her Cambridge entrance exams, but Alice kept summoning her to the lab for little briefings from Helena. She was supposed to relay certain urgent messages to Sasha on their mother's behalf: "She must understand that she is jeopardizing not only her academic future but her entire mental development" . . . "You must make her see that so far from being her enemy, as she seems to imagine, I am trying to stop her from doing irrevocable damage to herself." Instead, Isabel went and pleaded with Sasha to tell her what was wrong. "Poor Issy, doesn't understand a fucking thing, does she," Sasha said, her face stony with contempt.

On the day the headmistress phoned to say Sasha hadn't shown up (though Mark had driven her to the school door as usual), Isabel was summoned yet again, but this time Helena began by reassuring her that she'd been a perfectly satisfactory infant, even quite advanced for her age. Then she got to the point. Marvelous though he'd been in the war, she said, she'd realized that Isabel's father was not the ideal man to sire her children. Not an intellect of the first order, and she couldn't count on being lucky a second time. "There were many men like that, they performed the most extraordinary feats of bravery, they really were transformed, but once it was over they sank back into ordinariness again. Rather sad really to have passed one's peak so young. Not that there's anything sad about your father. Such a cheerful person."

Fortunately, she went on, she had some very remarkable friends. She hoped Isabel understood her meaning.

That was one of the times Isabel really hoped she was getting things wrong.

She had been perfectly honest with Roger, Helena went on, she'd assured him he'd have no obligation to the child, Teddy would assume it was his—here Isabel interrupted her; she'd rather not hear any more, she said, she couldn't listen to this. But Helena swatted that away. "I was simply offering him a chance for his genes to survive him." Roger was the object of the actress's question, the time she'd asked Isabel if she thought that man over there was drunk or merely vile: a fellow of All Souls, a frequent panelist on *The Brains Trust*, universally described as brilliant. Isabel had always been a little afraid of him; she'd hated the mocking way he talked to her father when her father tried to engage him in conversation: "A very interesting article in the paper the other day, by a terribly clever chap who thinks we'll be colonizing Mars in the not too distant future," her father would say, and Roger would inquire loudly, so everyone could share the joke, just when this great event would occur, or how exactly the clever chap knew.

Now Helena's voice changed, she became girlish and confiding. Did Isabel remember a man called Geoffrey Stonemarsh, she asked, and seemed annoyed that she didn't. Isabel had adored him, she said, he used to put her on his shoulders and take her for walks in the garden. He'd been so strong, she remembered, smiling dreamily, and yet so sweet, and eager. There was something very innocent about him, she said meaningfully, from which Isabel deduced he'd been a virgin. Being a virgin herself, she told me wryly, and in a panic at having to hear all this, she stood and said she was leaving, but Helena blocked her way, gripping her arm hard. "Don't be so childish," she said, there was a good reason she was telling the story now.

She had sent Isabel's father away, to see the solicitors in London; she had even given the servants the night off. They'd had a magical time together, she said; she'd given him tea in a glass, in the Russian style, and told him about her mother. And he had told her about his childhood on the Isle of Man, and about his younger sister, how clever she was, she was studying maths at Bristol. He still missed the sea, he said, so they went there the next morning, after their magical night, and made love again in her favorite spot on the sands. "Why do I have to know all this?" Isabel protested. She wanted her to understand, Helena said, that her decision was not untinged with sentiment.

Did Geoffrey Stonemarsh also know that his genes had been perpetuated, Isabel asked, and Helena said no, soon after that last visit to Sidworth, he'd left the country, to take up a post in Melbourne, and she hadn't wanted to inform him in a letter. Now, however, having acquired a wife and two children while in Australia, he was back in England, in a professorship at Manchester.

In fact, she said, he was doing some very remarkable work in genetics, people said he was bound to get the Nobel one of these days. "It's time Sasha understood what sort of genes she's carrying. You have to speak to her."

And why must Isabel do it?

Because, Helena said majestically, she would take it much better coming from Isabel, Sasha was too implacably hostile to her to listen to anything she had to say. ("Actually, I think she was a bit afraid of Sasha just then.")

She wouldn't do it, Isabel said hysterically, she couldn't, it was a terrible thing to ask of her, and besides, who knew what the shock would do to Sasha, she was so fragile right then. Very well, Helena said, she'd have no choice but to send Sasha away. "I cannot have my work disrupted like this." She picked up a brochure from her lab table, from a clinic for disturbed adolescents; she'd already spoken to a prominent expert, she said, who'd advised that electric shock therapy proved very effective in such cases. You can't do that, Isabel said, her voice cracking, you'll destroy her, but Helena said she most certainly could, it was precisely what she'd do if Isabel refused to cooperate. And was she supposed to tell Julian too, Isabel asked wildly, why not, maybe she could go to Harrow and break the news about Roger. "Don't be tiresome," Helena said.

In the end Isabel caved in, and the very next day went to Sasha to explain about her precious chromosomes. "I'd been up half the night rehearsing my little speech, trying to cast the story in the best possible light. I said how Mother had wanted a special child, and that's what Sasha was, she'd always been special, but she just stared at me with her mad red eyes. 'So Mum was putting it about, that's what you're telling me,' she said. 'And she calls me a slut.' Then she started to laugh, she was rocking back and forth on the bed laughing.

"Later she came to my room to ask if he knew about her, and I had to tell her he didn't, he'd been in Australia when she was born. 'So where is he now?' she asked, and when I told her she made a face. 'If he's such a genius, he ought to be at Oxbridge.' It just shows, doesn't it, that she was Mother's daughter to the last. An intellectual snob. 'Still,' she said, 'maybe I'll go look him up. Scare the hell out of him.'"

Isabel was in her first month at Cambridge when Sasha phoned to announce that she'd seen him. "It was late at night, she told the college porter it was an emergency and made him fetch me to the phone. So there I was, in my nightgown, standing in the freezing hallway in my bare feet, talking in a whisper so I wouldn't wake anyone up. She'd gone to his office at the university and confronted him. 'I even took out a little notebook and pretended to take notes,' she said. 'I asked him how old his grandparents were when they died, all sorts of shit like that. Whether there was any cancer in the family, heart disease, the whole bit. I did everything but examine his teeth.'"

And then, it seemed, he told her about his sister, the one who had been studying maths at Bristol when she was conceived. "Her name is Sally, and guess what? She's completely barking, she's been in and out of the bin for years. What kind of balls-up was that? I ask you. Little bit negligent about her research, Mum was that time. One of these days I should really ferret out the auntie, take her for a stroll or a hit of acid or something. We'd probably have a fabulous time together."

The next time Sasha phoned it was from a private clinic in Dorset: she had slit her wrists at the school for delinquents that Helena had sent her to, and been remanded there under court order. "But she'd phoned to reminisce. Even when she was four years old she used to be nostalgic for the snowdrops when they went. Or the snow when it melted. Or the nursery chair that had broken. That night she wanted to talk about Bax the donkey, how he grieved when Sam the mule died, because they'd always been pastured together.

"Then she said a girl at the clinic reminded her of Maddy—the same pale skin, she said, with a flush under it, and she wore her hair pulled back the same way. I'd forgotten that, about Maddy's skin, but she always remembered everything. She'd been thinking how bad I must have felt when Maddy died, she said, she was sorry, and did I ever find out why she did it."

"So did you tell her?"

She shook her head. "There didn't seem much point in piling on more revelations about Mother's love life. 'I realized today she was the first person I ever knew who died,' she said. 'Maybe I've been missing her ever since. Do you think that could be what's wrong with me, I'm grieving for Maddy? Like Bax and Sam?' It might not be Maddy she was grieving for, I said, maybe she was just grieving, and she got angry with me: people had to grieve *for* something, she said, nobody could just grieve, except maybe God. And then she said good night and hung up.

"For years she went back and forth to those clinics: two months out, three, once as long as six, but it never lasted. She'd have a bad trip on acid, she'd stay awake for days writing out equations or trying to decode the signals she was getting from weather reports or pop lyrics or railway timetables. It was as if her mind was being stretched farther and farther, she said, way outside her, right to where infinity started, she couldn't pull it back. First they called her schizo-phrenic, but later the diagnosis changed; she was manic-depressive, they said, except that didn't quite fit either, because of the delusions. The voices telling her she had to die. Schizoaffective disorder was the one that stuck, everyone could agree on that, it covered all her symptoms. But naming it didn't cure her. They kept trying her on different pills, the latest drug, the miracle worker, only there were no miracles, so they'd revert to the old ones again, Thorazine, or lithium, in some new incarnation. They'd tweak her dosage, switch from Jungian to art therapy to Gestalt, give her rag dolls to stab, with photos of our faces on them. And for a day or a week or a month it seemed to work: she was all better now, she'd tell me, she'd finally found it, the peace that passeth understanding. But the voices always came back."

Nine

The second time I went to Sidworth, I drove down with Isabel on a rainy November morning, and when we got to the house the door was flung open by a wild-eyed, disheveled young woman in a ratty bathrobe. "Thank God you're here. I've been trying to reach you on the phone all morning." This was Pauline, Helena's latest secretary; the reason she'd been phoning was that Helena had tried suicide the night before and then changed her mind. Having swallowed a whole bottle of sleeping pills, she'd phoned the ambulance at one in the morning and been taken to Barnstaple Hospital, where her stomach had been pumped. At eight a.m., before the doctor arrived to prevent her, she had dressed herself and called a cab to take her home.

"Is she all right?" Isabel asked, and Pauline said furiously, "Of course she's not all right. She should never have come back, she could barely stagger up to her bedroom. But she won't let me bring in a nurse. You've got to speak to her. I can't cope with this, I can't be responsible."

She turned and marched up the stairs, with Isabel, mouthing apologies at me, hurrying after. I wondered if I could possibly find my way to Isabel's cottage and wait for her there. But just then Pauline leaned over the banister. "Would you come upstairs now please," she said, sounding cross. "She wants to see you."

So I ascended the grand staircase and we entered the bedroom together. "You may go now, Pauline," Helena said. She was propped up in bed against tapestry pillows, in what looked like an Elizabethan bodice, embroidered with flowers, and a crimson turban that set off the greenish white of her skin. The effect should have been comic, but somehow it wasn't. "Come here," she said, and then, "Awfully kind of you to travel all this way to be with my daughter," in a tone that implied I couldn't have many calls on my time. "But then I gather you're a very dear friend."

I mumbled something noncommittal, which she ignored, gesturing toward a battered velvet chaise longue, strewn with books and offprints, opposite the bed. "You may sit down." I perched on the edge, so as not to disturb any of the piles. "Just sweep those things off, go ahead, Pauline can tidy them up later." And when I had removed just enough of them to sit back a little, piling them carefully on the carpet, "You're very polite, aren't you. For an American."

"How are you feeling?" I asked lamely.

"Perfectly fine, thanks. Extremely well rested. I suppose it's back to the rat poison now." And when I looked startled, "It's used as a blood thinner, did you not know that?"

No, I said, I didn't. "Of course you're too young to concern yourself with coagulation of the blood." For a moment there was silence. Then she said, "I understand you once cohabited with my son."

Isabel, who'd been standing by the bed, went to the fireplace and started fiddling with the stones and feathers on the mantel.

"That's right."

"Are you still in regular contact with him?"

"Not even irregular contact." She grimaced, whether in response to my half-assed joke or because she was in pain I wasn't sure.

"Would you hand me that glass?" The water dribbled down her chin, though she seemed not to notice. Her turban had slid down on one side and was snagged on her left ear, but she seemed not to notice that either. She fumbled the glass back to the bedside table, half on and half off. Isabel came and moved it to safety, while Helena glared at her.

"I don't need you and your little friend here ministering to me, thank you. I still have a perfectly fine brain, and I intend to use it. Tomorrow I shall begin work on a paper I've been mulling over for months."

That was all well and good, Isabel said, but she was still going to hire a nurse, at least for a few days. "For Pauline's sake, if not yours. She's terribly worried about you, she can't be responsible for your well-being."

"Nonsense." She turned to me. "What do you know about eugenics?" And when I said Nothing, "That's precisely my point. Thanks to Herr Hitler, the very word is taboo. Would it surprise you to learn that before the war George Bernard Shaw and H. G. Wells and all the leading intellectuals were involved with it? Keynes headed up the Eugenics Society, people forget that. The Webbs were mad for it. Churchill too. Bertrand Russell proposed that the state should issue different grades of procreation tickets depending on a person's abilities."

"All right, Mother," Isabel said. "We can talk about this later. I'm going downstairs to phone the nursing agency now."

"Not yet. Another minute, and I'm done." She addressed me again. "The *Annals of Eugenics* became the *Annals of Human Genetics*. The Galton Chair of Eugenics became the Chair of Genetics."

"It's almost two o'clock; if I don't phone the agency now, it may be too late to get anyone today."

"My daughter seems to think I should give up mental activity altogether. Quite the contrary. This little episode has made me feel how urgent it is to put my ideas in circulation. I may even write a short book."

I made what I hoped was an encouraging noise.

"I'm not suggesting we should punish the weak, or even the undesirables. Far from it. But should they be allowed to go on propagating indefinitely? It's a question that at least needs to be asked. And the more the science of genetics has developed, the more it should be put to practical use. Before it's too late." By this point I had ceased making little murmurs of assent; I just stared. "Galton's argument was that the quality of the race could be painlessly improved through selective breeding. Is that such an ignoble aim?"

She shot a quick glance at Isabel; it must have occurred to her that Isabel would be remembering her own breeding experiments. "The situation is entirely different now from what it once was, there's so much data available. And the necessary systems have been established. In America they've got Nobel Prize winners donating their sperm, and women are queuing up to bear their children."

"That's not how I'd want to conceive a child," Isabel muttered.

"You went in for hybrid vigor. Nothing wrong with that. Still, I suspect you were relieved when the child turned out so fair. The odds were against that, as you know."

"I wasn't a bit relieved. I've always wished Lucy looked more like her father."

"That's just sentiment talking."

"I think it's called love, Mother."

"Nonsense. You were always prey to sentiment. Even as a child." And back to me, "What makes nurses so intolerable is that they always speak to one as though one's mentally impaired. Do I appear mentally impaired to you?"

"You may be the least mentally impaired person I've ever met. But you should still really get a nurse."

"Your little chum is very staunch, isn't she? Mrs. Tweedie"—that was the current housekeeper—"can look after me."

"She can*not*," Isabel said, roused to fury at last. "She is not trained, she's not prepared, it's absolutely unfair to ask it of her. You've already had one stroke, and you've just had some very nasty substances pumped out of your body. Who knows what the aftereffects will be? Besides, if you refuse the nurse, Pauline will leave, and then you'll have nobody to help with your paper."

"Or your book," I said sweetly.

"Pauline is no use to me anyway. A first at Oxford, and the mind of a squid. Thank God I never went to university."

"That's not what you said the last time I was here."

"I was giving her the benefit of the doubt. But magnanimity must give way to truth. And truth, by the way, is just what she won't acknowledge. Not when it interferes with her sense of moral rectitude."

"All right, then, I'll tell her she can leave."

Helena shut her eyes. "All right, all right. Go and make your phone call. You're wearing me out with all this bickering." But when I made to follow Isabel, she called me back. "Just a minute, please. I have something to discuss with you." I sat back down with a sick feeling in my stomach: was she going to ask me what Julian had said about her?

It was nothing so predictable. "Are you aware," she asked, gripping my hand, "that my son is a drug addict?" And when I objected that I'd never seen him take drugs, she said frantically, "It has to be that," her nails digging into my flesh. "Nothing else could account for his monstrous unkindness. His mind is diseased, that much is plain, and what else can have caused it? There was nothing in his genes, he never showed any signs of mental illness. Never. I would have known, I would have seen." Her voice cracked; in that moment she was wholly human, a sick old woman grieving over her wayward son. Then, with an effort, she recovered, she lay back on the pillows, exhausted, and told me to leave her.

By the time the nurse arrived—a stout friendly woman with an impenetrable accent that Isabel said was Cornish—I was hoping we could get out of there and relax over a bottle of wine in the cottage kitchen. But there were daughter-of-the-house duties to be performed: first in the kitchen, where Mrs. Tweedie served us crustless fish-paste sandwiches and walnut cake and sympathized tactfully with the situation, while Isabel sympathized with her in turn, and asked after her grandchildren, and in general was irritatingly charming in the way she'd been with me the first time I met her.

Pauline required further attention. Mrs. Tweedie brought a tray of tea and homemade scones and jam into the morning room and switched on the fringed lamps for us. "I was over the moon when I heard I'd got this job," Pauline said glumly. "I remember rushing over to my friends' rooms and bursting in saying, 'Guess what!' And everybody at St. Hilda's hugging me, saying how lucky I was."

Isabel put a scone on a little flowered plate, with a pat of butter, and handed it to her. "I know, it

must have been a terrible shock, all this. Really horrid for you."

"Oh, it's not just this latest business," Pauline said.
"It's all the talk of mongrel races. Crossbreeding." She
bit into her scone. "Has she mentioned that to you?"

"Not in those words. But she does seem keen on
the subject of eugenics."

"She's been on about it for weeks. It's fascist science,
that's what, it's diabolical, I refuse to be a party to it."

There was a cough; the Cornish nurse stood in the
doorway.

"Sorry to disturb you, Miss, but your mum would
like a word with you upstairs. I'm afraid she's not set-
tling very well." Isabel went off, and Pauline turned
to me.

"I don't believe for a moment she was serious about
offing herself. She's just in a snit about this Christmas
business."

"Oh, do you think so?" I asked, with no idea what
the Christmas business was.

"I know so." She sucked on a strand of her hair,
gazing moodily out the window, where the light was
already fading to pink over the hills. "Who'd ever
think you'd come to such a beautiful place and leave it
a bitter old cynic?"

I pointed out that she wasn't exactly old, and I
doubted she'd stay bitter forever. "What are you?
Twenty-one?"

"Twenty-two. But I feel like I'm a hundred and
five."

Later, in the peace of the cottage, sitting at the kitchen table with the promised bottle of wine, I asked what Pauline had meant by the Christmas business. It turned out to be a Grand Guignol version of a family tug of war. Helena wanted Isabel and Lucy there for the holiday, Isabel had been holding out. She wanted time at home with Lucy before Lucy went off with her friends to Guernsey for a New Year's party: "Half-term was such a disaster. And Sasha's coming to stay from Christmas Eve through Boxing Day, while Daphne goes to her family. You're invited too, by the way, if you have nothing better planned."

Helena had said she could bring Sasha along, but Sasha's last visit to Sidworth had been a nightmare, she told me; she'd waved a bicycle pump at Pauline and told Mrs. Tweedie she smelled of death. "Anyway, as she points out, Mother never particularly wanted us here for Christmas when it was full of her friends. Only now there are hardly any left: either they're dead, or they've quarreled, or they're too infirm to travel." Apparently Roger had keeled over and died in the Codrington that summer, while the countess had fallen into an empty swimming pool at her Dordogne estate and cracked her skull open. "So Mother has developed a late-life yearning for the company of her children."

She'd planned instead to drive to Bedales for the end-of-term play, in which Lucy was playing the love interest, the last woman in town to metamorphose into a beast, in Ionesco's *Rhinoceros*, and drive back to London with her afterward.

But then Lucy phoned her in tears: Helena had written to her and told her she'd be spending Christmas alone. "Isn't it too sad, Mum, to think of Granny there all by herself...We can't let that happen, can we, specially when it'll probably be her last Christmas on earth, she said so herself. That Pauline has left, did you know, Granny said she'd even threatened her. Isn't it awful? They showed a film about it at school, about old people being bullied, and lying in their own pee and everything. Sometimes their carers even beat them up. So we're putting on our play in an old people's home in Petersfield next term."

Not only that, but Helena had told her that Ionesco was a friend of hers, that he'd come to Sidworth once. "I should have told her about the play earlier, she said, maybe he would have come, he only lives in Paris. Wouldn't that have been awesome?"

And so Isabel drove Lucy and Sasha down to Sidworth on the twenty-second. On the twenty-fifth she phoned me, to see if I was doing okay on my own. While she'd been playing skivvy, she told me, Mrs. Tweedie having been given the holiday off, and cooking the Christmas turkey in the ancient Aga, along with a nutloaf for Lucy, who had gone vegetarian, Sasha was barricaded in her room, playing scratchy old Sex Pistols and Screamers records on her ancient gramophone. Meanwhile Lucy was bringing in buckets of coal to feed the fire in the study, where she was ensconced with her grandmother, listening to tales of dear Eojen ("You must pronounce it in the Romanian fashion") and dear Roland and dear André.

"No mention, though, of the Webbs and Bertrand Russell and their views on the breeding of undesirables. I suppose she realized that wouldn't go over well with Lucy."

So: Game, set, match to Helena.

Ten

At Stony Brook I had developed a certain scorn for the glossy rich girls whose lunch plates I had to clear away, wearing a hairnet and overalls, for $3.75 an hour, and not just because of their habit of stubbing out their cigarettes in their leftover cheesecake. They were always shrieking with laughter, they had such an air of sucking greedily at all the goodies the world had to offer.

Now I realized that, for all their fancy clothes, they hadn't been truly *posh*, whereas of course Isabel was, very posh, though I think she made conscientious efforts to play it down. But sometimes, if she was excited, or in fervent agreement with something I'd said, she slipped out of her pleasantly neutral accent and reverted to something closer to her mother's. Once I was telling her about a show of roses at Kew Gardens I was writing up for some magazine, and she said, waving a rare cigarette, "Oh, it sounds too too riveting." Later, when I came to introduce her to my new friends, there was always a subtle shift in their manner around her, a heightening of attention, as though metaphorically they were sitting up straighter.

Which may be part of what she'd loved about Greece, where she might not have been so easy to place, except as an Anglo. (I knew a little about that, feeling happily unplaceable in England.) But when she told me about it, it was always Stavros she talked about. It made me uneasy sometimes; she was so worshipful, telling me about his specialness, his wisdom: "At first I had this idea I was going to save him, heal him from his despair, only then I saw it wasn't despair, it wasn't some sickness in him but a kind of knowledge. A way of seeing things as they really were. Which I'd never had the courage for." Maybe that was true. But it felt strange that she rarely mentioned being happy with him. Nor was there any of that wild carefree Zorba-the-Greek-dancing-barefoot-on-the-sand stuff (though she did say he took her on his battered old Vespa to watch the sun setting over the sea).

Instead he had set out to re-educate her. The first time they met, in the foreign-language bookshop where he worked, she had asked for a new translation of Cavafy, and he had told her Cavafy was a fascist. No he wasn't, she said, shocked, but he insisted: yes, he was a fascist, he had accepted a medal from a fascist dictator. Furthermore, Mr. T. S. Eliot—she was carrying a copy of his plays—was a fascist also; did all English ladies have a liking for fascists? He could not agree to order her a copy of the poems of Mr. Ezra Pound, if that was what she'd like next. She laughed as she told me this, but her eyes were shining, as though it were proof of what a pure soul he was. Like Wittgenstein or someone.

A few days later, as she was crossing the street, he came around the corner on his Vespa, spattering mud all over her skirt; dismounting, he helped to brush it off—"This is a sin against civilization, to dirty an English lady's clothing"—and then he asked her if she'd like to come for a coffee. That was the beginning. But for months, she said, he never talked to her about what he considered his real life: she knew about the other parts, his architecture studies at the Polytechnic, his work in the bookshop ten hours a week, but he never told her where he went on the evenings he wasn't with her.

When she'd registered for her fellowship at the British School, she'd had to sign a form promising not to interfere in the country's politics, but there had been so many forms; she didn't give it much thought, nobody at the school ever mentioned it. If there was military music blaring from the cafés, if there were posters everywhere of a soldier emerging from the stomach of a phoenix, it all seemed part of the same foreignness as the street markets, with their piles of orange spices, and the bells that rang at all hours in the churches. Men in uniform, guns slung over their shoulders, patrolled the avenues, but the young ones could also be seen strolling with girls in the royal gardens, admiring the swans. To her, she said, the soldiers seemed less sinister than the priests, with their long beards and black robes; the priests never smiled at her, but the soldiers did.

Then, when Stavros was very late meeting her one night, and wouldn't tell her why, she accused him of having another girlfriend; was that the reason, she asked, that sometimes, when she phoned him at his rooming house at a time they'd arranged, nobody could find him? At that he started shouting. What kind of a fool was she, he yelled, what Greece did she think she was living in, did she have any idea what was happening all around her? Or didn't the Brits care about that, they were too busy with fucking Simonides and fucking Minoan pottery to see what was going on under their noses. In the military prison at Aegina, he told her, they were burning young men's testicles, they were beating old men senseless; on the island of Giaros, they were herding children and pregnant women into cages too small even to lie down in, and leaving them there to bake in the sun.

"And then I remembered the man at Madame Evangelides's flat—the woman who was teaching me modern Greek. She never strayed from the subject at hand, she only talked to me about the formation of the aorist subjunctive in the second conjugation, or the relative versus the absolute superlative. But one afternoon there was a knock at her door, and a man with a squashed nose and one eye swollen shut slid inside. As soon as he saw me, he started to back out, but Madame caught hold of his sleeve and walked him down the corridor, toward the rear of the flat. A minute later she came back with a saucer of quince preserves and we went on with the lesson as though nothing had happened. I assumed he was her ne'er-do-well son, or her drunken nephew or something. God. How could I have been so stupid?"

Soon a resistance cell was holding meetings at the flat her mother had rented for her in Kolonaki—her idea, her way of keeping Stavros safe, or at least safer. Nobody expected the revolution to be planned where the rich women shopped, and besides, her building even had a rear entrance. One by one, the others could slip in the back door and up the stairs after dark, though Eleni, also an architecture student, refused; wearing short spangly skirts and fishnet stockings, her face smeared with bright red rouge, she rang the front bell. Dressing like a tart was the best disguise, she said, everyone knew that all the tarts in the city were fascists. Later Eleni would be Lucy's unofficial godmother.

At first Isabel shut herself in the bedroom when they came, to give them privacy. But one night Eleni knocked on the door and said she'd brought some homemade retsina from her grandfather's village, why didn't she come out and drink with them? The next time she made herself useful by helping Grigoris, the sternest Marxist of the group (a banker's son, Stavros had told her, the richest of them all), unjam the primitive mimeograph machine they used to print their leaflets; it squatted permanently by then on what had been her dining room table. A week later, when a salesclerk demanded to see Eleni's ID because she was asking for suspicious amounts of paper, she came to Isabel: "Tell them it's to perform *The Bacchae* at the British School, you will all dance naked for this, but first there must be printed many copies of the script. Make a pretty English smile. 'Yes madam,' they'll say, 'certainly madam' ... born slaves they are." And that was exactly what happened.

Then it was spring, the air was full of scented mildness, and her period was ten days late.

She said nothing to Stavros, who would accuse her, rightly, of carelessness: she had neglected to take her pills for several days running. She would have to return to England, get an abortion. Maybe she wouldn't come back. She would leave him a note, saying the rent was paid through June, saying it was for the best, saying she loved him, or not saying it, in case he didn't want to hear that. Not since the spring when Maddy died had she felt so lonely, she told me, as though surrounded by too much space, and the light was hurting her eyes.

A month before, a letter had come from Stavros's mother in Patras, announcing the birth of his sister's second child. He'd crumpled it up and thrown it across the room. "And this is supposed to make me hopeful," he said bitterly, "yes, our children are our future, the world is being born afresh, let us rejoice for the little miracle God has sent." Now there she was, hormones surging through her body, gazing foolishly at a baby kicking its fat little heels against its stroller, a boy with curly dark hair like Stavros's chasing a ball in the royal gardens, conviction growing in her against her will, against all good sense, that she wasn't going to abort this baby. She was going to have it. Somehow. Somewhere. In England, because there it would not be so shocking, things had changed, not just rock singers but lady doctors, lady dons were giving birth to bastards.

When she could no longer keep the secret—he'd stood in the bathroom doorway two mornings running, watching her throw up in the toilet—it took him about half an hour of pacing the living room, running his hands through his hair, to stop muttering ominously and begin to laugh: what a wonderful baby it would be, a really extraordinary baby, his and hers. (It just went to show, Eleni said, rolling her eyes, that he was a typical Greek male after all.) Throughout her pregnancy his black moods were not as frequent, he read the poems of Seferis aloud as she chopped onions, he even hammered bits of wood into a cradle. Long before the baby could have developed hearing he put his head against her stomach and sang the songs of his childhood: "Cloudy Sunday, you are like my heart." The singing continued into the first few months of Lucy's life; when she woke in the night, he'd bring her into their bed and croon to her. "He never got bored with singing those songs to her, which was strange, since he was easily bored. Not someone known for his patience."

People were in and out of the flat all the time, unannounced, no peace, no order. She wasn't cut out for any of it, she had always craved silence, her realest life had gone on inside her head. And now, when she was exhausted as never before, her nerves on edge, looking after a colicky baby, and then, when Lucy was asleep, checking every few minutes to make sure she was still breathing, this craziness. But there were moments of pure joy too, she said, the three of them lying together in the early mornings, and even beyond that, she told me, she was conscious of feeling more hopeful, less afraid of the dark center, than ever before. It seemed impossible that Stavros and the others, all those dozens of people meeting in cellars across the city, ferrying fugitives between safe houses, smuggling false papers inside the prisons, wouldn't triumph in the end. History was on their side, they were doing something great and necessary. "Whereas I'd never been part of anything that mattered," she said. "I'd never even thought of trying to change things. All my silly little struggles had only ever been about myself."

How could I answer that? Don't be so hard on yourself? So I said nothing, I let her go on with the story. But it made me remember what Julian had said, about her gazing raptly at Stavros, while he hardly looked at her.

As Lucy's first birthday approached, he became restless and nervy, pacing the flat, striking his forehead with his fist and declaring more and more trivial mishaps a "katastrophi"—a broken corkscrew, an exam on which he'd done less than perfectly. Once that had been his word for recounting to her, proudly, the history of his family, which was also the history of Greece in the twentieth century: a series of catastrophes. (His father's great-grandfather had been hanged by the Turks during the War of Independence; his mother's family had been part of the mass expulsion from

Smyrna; her brother, part of the resistance during the German occupation, was shot after a collaborator cousin turned him in. His father's two brothers had been on opposing sides during the civil war.) Now he snapped at her for leaving the butter out of the fridge, for using the wrong olive oil; it was all she could do, exhausted as she was, not to burst out sobbing. She worried that he was growing tired of domesticity, even of Lucy's demands, what her mother would call the whole shooting match. He was no longer singing. She could feel the tension in his body. They hardly ever made love. But after the uprising at the law school that February, after posters and leaflets against the government started proliferating even on the broad avenues leading to the parliament building, she woke one night to find him leaning over the cradle he'd made and whispering to their sleeping child that everything was about to change, she was going to be *eleftheria*, free, like her name.

In the third week of November Eleni phoned just as Stavros was about to leave for a stint at the bookshop and told him about a demonstration under way at the Polytechnic. "Now it begins," he said exultantly, when he hung up. "So you'll go," she said, and he nodded. Should she phone Themis at the bookshop, she asked, and make some excuse, but he brushed this away impatiently, he was already heading for the door.

All that day she kept the radio on, and then, suddenly, new voices came through—the voices of Polytechnic students who had locked themselves in and rigged up a radio station somehow. Over and over, the same three voices, none of which she recognized, urged the public to rise up against the colonels. "People of Greece, join with us . . . we are unarmed . . . our only weapon is our faith in freedom."

Stavros didn't come back that night, nor the next. On the morning of the third day, she put Lucy into the fluffy red coat Helena had sent and pushed her stroller to the Polytechnic. Crowds had gathered outside the gates, shabby men of all ages, old women in black, with headscarves, the men stamping their feet, shouting out support for the students. But now she was a foreigner again, without Stavros and Eleni and Grigoris she had no place there, people looked at her suspiciously, and the shouting made Lucy cry. She tried to tell her it was all right, it wasn't bad shouting, it was cheering, Lucy should cheer too. "Let's sing a song," she said, "the one about cloudy Sunday," but Lucy only cried harder. She took her home and gave her lunch; then she listened to the radio some more, the crackling voices fading in and out, exhorting their fellow Athenians to join them. She put Lucy down for her nap and fell asleep in the armchair. When she woke the radio was blaring static; no amount of fiddling with the knobs could bring the voices back. Only the official stations, with the same martial music, the same old folk tunes they had always played.

After breakfast, she dressed Lucy in a hat and mittens as well as her red coat—"even in Athens, November can be chilly"—and went downstairs. Her landlady was standing in the doorway, talking to a woman from the building opposite. She had always greeted Stavros politely when she came to collect the rent, she had cooed over Lucy and called her an angel, a little darling. But there was a look of malice on her face as she asked Isabel if she'd heard the news. What news? Isabel said stupidly, and the other two started talking over each other: the tanks had entered the Polytechnic just before dawn, the students had been taken away. "Thank God," the landlady said, crossing herself. "We don't need any more riots, we had enough of those with the Communists. Put them all in the army, that will teach them respect." The other woman spat on the sidewalk. "Prison is where they belong," she said. "Lock them up, maybe that will knock some sense into them."

When Isabel told the fat man at Security Police Headquarters on Sofias that she was there to inquire about one of the students, he laughed heartily, he patted her hand and winked at Lucy. "Take your little girl and go home." Her former professor at the British School went stony-faced when she knocked on his door and pleaded for help; he could not interfere in the politics of another country, he said. In desperation, she phoned the consul, a friend of her mother's whom Helena had urged her to get in touch with when she first arrived, but he was out of the country, they told her, shooting in Scotland. She went back with Lucy to the Polytechnic, deserted now, the iron gates dangling off their hinges, canisters of tear gas strewn around, the smell still lingering, burning her throat. People hurried by with handkerchiefs held to their mouths. A bent old woman in a black dress and shawl, looking as if she'd just come down from the mountains—to search for her son, her grandson?—stooped down painfully and picked up one of the blood-smeared leaflets that lay on the ground, examining both sides, as though it might tell her what she needed to know. Isabel wondered if it had been printed on the paper she'd bought.

For a whole week she could learn nothing. And then Eleni came, entering by the back way this time, her miniskirt abandoned for jeans. One of her eyes was swollen shut, her arm was in a makeshift sling, bright red and orange. "What happened to you?" Isabel cried, and she shrugged. "The same thing that happened to everyone else. This"—she pointed to her eye—"was a rifle butt. This"—gesturing at the sling with her other hand—"was a truncheon. I don't have time to give the whole story. I can't stay long." Someone had seen Stavros loaded into an ambulance, she said—the soldiers had shot at the tires—before the final invasion by the tanks. Nobody knew where he'd been taken. "I didn't see him myself, there were fires everywhere, the guys were pissing on them to put them out. I couldn't see much of anything. But I trust the person who told me. I'll let you know as soon as I hear." She kissed Isabel on both cheeks and ran down the stairs.

And so she waited, she waited. She had Lucy to look after, she couldn't afford to fall apart completely. She cried only at night, when Lucy was asleep. Sometimes she managed to sleep herself. On the fourth day she phoned his mother, who had come on the train from Patras six months before to meet Lucy, though only once, since she did not share Helena's unorthodox views on marriage. In her eyes, Isabel had brought disgrace on the family: thanks to the colonels, Lucy had been born a bastard—civil marriages were outlawed, and the church would not perform a marriage to a Protestant. "So no godparents could reject Satan in Lucy's name by spitting in the church doorway."

Nor, as Stavros's concubine, was she entitled to make inquiries. But his mother was; her cousin, she said—the collaborator?—was in Athens seeking information. She would be in touch when they knew anything. "You understand?" she asked sharply, several times, and Isabel wasn't sure if she meant, Do you understand my Greek? or Do you understand what this might mean? Or even, Do you understand how crazy he was, my son, to put himself in that danger? "And I couldn't say he was right to do it, it was for his country, it was in the cause of freedom. Because I didn't really believe in freedom and heroism and the shining light of truth right then, I didn't believe in anything. I just wanted Lucy to have a father. I was a little bourgeoise after all."

She told herself he must be a prisoner somewhere, she was waiting for the British consul to return from his grouse shoot and make his own inquiries: her mother promised to talk to him herself.

And then Stavros's sister, whom she'd never met, phoned, her voice hostile, as though what had happened was somehow Isabel's fault. They'd had bad news, she said bluntly. His name was on a list of the dead. That same week the government was toppled, but not to usher in democracy: the generals had seized power, there would be no referendum, no *eleftheria*. Nothing worth dying for. Their child had been made fatherless to no purpose.

And still she thought there might be a mistake, if she just stayed put he might show up, bruised and bloody but alive. The following month his sister phoned again: they had filled out the forms and paid the fees, his body was on its way to Patras. She made no mention of Isabel coming to the interment.

When Eleni emerged from hiding, a week later, she insisted they must hold an *agrypnia*, a wake, for his absent body, with a *koliva*, the traditional sugared cake for the dead, though they could not go from door to door in Kolonaki offering spoonfuls to the neighbors. Eleni's eye was only a little puffy by then, her arm was in a neat white splint. The tattered remnants of the group—the ones who were still alive, still able to walk, not locked up somewhere—came to the flat bearing plates of fava and stuffed vine leaves and bottles of cheap retsina to go with Eleni's cake. They kissed Isabel once, twice, three times; they threw their arms around each other, weeping. A woman she had never seen before sat cross-legged on the floor, under the poster of Lambrakis, the resisters' hero, rocking back and forth and wailing like the chorus in *The Trojan Women*: she could have written a paper about it, Isabel said, for her seminar on classical drama. She was the only one with dry eyes, a dry throat.

"Once, when I was pregnant, I went with Eleni and Stavros and the others to a cellar in Kaisariani where they played the old wailing rebetiko music. The Germans had banned it as a threat to order, it was too wild and sorrowful, and then the junta banned it too. Sometimes the police came and smashed the players' bouzoukis. But that night in Kaisariani there were no police, no soldiers, only old men and young students. And everyone was smoking, and singing, and the men were dancing together. I must have looked totally out of place, the only foreigner, but I've never had such a sense of what you might call universal brotherhood. At one point I whispered to Eleni, 'I think I must have been Greek in some other incarnation.' I meant it as a joke, I wasn't serious, but she threw out her arms and said, 'Of course! Of course you were! I knew it from the first time I met you. Our little blonde Greek, like the ancients.'

"But that day I couldn't bear the smoke in my living room, all the smeared plates, and that woman moaning. I opened a window to let some air in, but the smell from outside was even worse, exhaust and day-old fish and burning plastic. And the loudspeaker on the corner was blaring martial music." She thought with longing, she said, of the green lawns of England, the pale yellow roses climbing the orchard wall at Sidworth. The white eyelet sheets of her childhood. She never wanted to hear anyone cry again. Two weeks later she and Lucy were on a plane to London.

Eleven

About Lucy she was often mock-despairing, about Sasha the despair felt real.

"The offspring has decided I'm what she calls a saddo," she'd tell me dryly. "I think it's partly embarrassment, it seems all her friends at Bedales have these terribly exciting mothers who do conceptual art and stencil the rooms of their houses in the south of France. Whereas I, according to her, lead such a dead boring life she worries about me...maybe I should move into a flat, she says, she hates to think of me sitting in that house all the time on my own. I keep telling her I'm perfectly fine, of course I miss her but really I'm fine with my life, and then she gives an enormous sigh and asks why I think I always have to be so selfless, it's really really icky, she says. Oh dear."

The note of amusement was rarely present when she was talking about Sasha.

Tuesday was the day she went to South Kensington, and when we met on Wednesday in the Reading Room I could almost gauge how things had gone from the look on her face. Often they went badly:

Sasha had refused to let her in, she'd stood on the other side of the door and shouted at her to go away; Sasha had sat there mutely the whole time; Sasha had accused her of patronizing her, she was like some Victorian do-gooder, she said, putting on her bonnet and visiting the poor. But however nasty she'd been, Isabel always made excuses. It was like listening to someone talk about her abusive boyfriend: he didn't mean it, he can't help it, he felt so bad afterward. There was no more talk of Sasha having turned the corner.

It seemed she kept going off her meds, because they made her fat, or woozy, or they dulled out her mind so much she bored herself. Then she'd go nuts again. So why didn't she just take the fucking pills? That was what the mean-minded Gurneyville side of me felt like saying. Also that what she needed was a kick up the ass. Only Isabel wasn't about to deliver it.

I did once suggest that maybe firmness rather than sympathy would work, maybe it would do Sasha good if people didn't cave in to her—trying to plant the idea that she was getting her rocks off making Isabel feel like shit—and she went all snooty on me: "I don't think you quite understand. She's not being willfully difficult, she's ill, she's genuinely, seriously ill; it's no good applying those sort of crude techniques of control...as though she were a dog I was training. I think we'd better drop the subject."

"And screw you too, lady," I muttered under my breath.

At which she reached over and touched my hand. "I'm sorry, really, that was horrid of me. Please forgive me."

So I did. Partly I was just bored with the whole thing, and probably jealous as well: all that love and worry Isabel expended on her, I wouldn't have minded some of that myself. But even more shameful, it was the idea of Harrods that stuck in my craw. Because when Sasha wasn't being mute or accusing, they'd go to Harrods, where she'd charge things on their mother's account. Mostly wildly impractical clothes, from the sound of it—red high-heeled sandals, a silk blouse with diamond cutouts—though one of her lines was that she couldn't look into mirrors for fear there'd be nobody there. Why did she buy clothes, then? And that line about mirrors: it sounded familiar—hadn't she taken it from some book?

I savored my righteous anger, the bitter taste of bile in my mouth. I told myself it wasn't for myself I felt indignant, but on behalf of my new friends, my worthy and wronged and erudite and impoverished friends, who would never in their lives get to charge satin sandals at Harrods.

Several times, while I'd waited to turn in my request slips at the Reading Room's central octagon, I'd exchanged smiles with a tall bony woman with bright red lipstick and ferocious-looking horn-rims. One day she was behind me in the cafeteria queue and knocked over her cup of coffee, which splashed all over my yellow sweater. She was so distressed, apologizing over and over, handing me napkin after napkin from the dispenser on the counter, that I couldn't be angry; it was a very old sweater, I told her, in fact I'd bought it at the Mind shop, it really didn't matter. "You're too kind," she said, and when we arrived at the cash register she invited me to sit with her and her friends at their table in the corner, which is how I increased my acquaintance in London by a factor of four.

It turned out they were all victims of Mrs. Thatcher's cuts to higher education, forced into early retirement by the academic equivalent of the Big Bang on the stock exchange the year before. The woman who'd ruined my sweater had been a reader in philosophy at one of the polytechnics until half her department was eliminated to make way for a degree course in marketing. The others, all men, were a particle physicist, a professor of French, and a historian specializing in the Wars of the Roses. All, though their prospects of ever finding other posts were dim, were diligently researching books in their field, which explained their constant presence in the Reading Room, though inadequate heating in their flats may also have been a factor.

Their faces in repose looked sallow and defeated, but laughter enlivened their features, there was nothing they enjoyed more than a good joke. Gleefully satirical about virtually everything, they refused to let any note of sadness in. Instead, making a great point of their advanced age compared to me—they were all in their fifties—they vied with each other in delivering Polonius-like injunctions: I must be sensible, and hardheaded, and find myself a rich husband as soon as possible—"some pooh-bah in the City, with lots of dosh . . . Or why not a sheikh, you can be his London wife, he won't be much trouble, he'll only show up perhaps three or four times a year."

Because, unlike Isabel, they were so obviously down at heel (literally—the state of the physicist's shoes was alarming), I found myself confessing, only the second time I joined them for lunch, about the Toby jugs and the cigarette picture cards. In the weeks that followed, much merriment was expended, over egg-and-cress sandwiches, on thinking up ridiculous subjects for *Art & Antiques*—Victorian kitty litter trays, Restoration spittoons.

But beyond all that, they took a protective interest in my welfare, putting such resources as they had at my disposal. The historian, whose eternal cardigans were so shapeless, so full of cigarette burns, they seemed like something out of a 1950s movie, reviewed occasionally for the *New Statesman*, and hooked me up with his editor there. The French professor, whose gold-rimmed spectacles slipped to the very end of his nose whenever he became animated, had a son at the *TLS* he persuaded to assign me an occasional review for the "In Brief" section—all on American subjects, though, which wounded me a little. I dashed off my articles for the antiques magazines and labored mightily over a five-hundred-word piece on a history of the WPA, for which I was paid twenty pounds.

The old notion of the literary life was still alive then, if just barely—at least it was to me, though my new friends assured me I was deluded, it was dead as the dodo, had been for some time. But it seemed to me they embodied the very ideal they were warning me against, something shabbier and more thrilling than mere glamour, an unworldly kind of striving in which failure was hardly relevant and unhappiness a perfectly reasonable price to pay. I was thirty-one years old, and had renounced all forms of romance, but it didn't occur to me to guard against exalted feelings about the dome of the Reading Room, or the sight of the handwritten manuscripts of "Kubla Khan" and *Jane Eyre*. Even the grubbiness of my bedsit and the leanness of my daily existence began to feel like points of honor. It was perversely exhilarating to turn my back on consumerism just as the rest of England was discovering its joys with a vengeance.

At Stony Brook I had "mother-sat" one weekend for a visiting economics professor from Portsmouth whose elderly mother was staying with him for a month; she was afraid to be left alone in his house while he was off at some conference. All her remarks were of an almost surreal banality, everything was described as "ever so nice," whether it was a Hostess Twinkie or her sister Edith's room in her nursing home in Dorset or the stewardess on her flight from London, who had given her an extra blanket. But somehow it was very soothing, listening to her; after a while I felt lulled rather than bored. On both Friday and Saturday evening she had sat knitting beside what she called the wireless, listening to the local station, and then clucking her tongue when the news came on—"Isn't it shocking, the things some people get up to, you wouldn't believe they could be so wicked, would you," or, alternatively, "the poor dear." At nine o'clock she went and made us cups of cocoa, which she brought out on a tray along with home-made shortbread, of which she ate just one, while I had to stop myself from finishing them off. "I suppose you think it's very silly of me, dear," she said, as we sat down to a Sunday meal she'd insisted on cooking without assistance, "not wanting to be alone here, but it's not the same in a foreign country, is it. And not being able to drive . . . it's ever so nice of you to have kept me company like this." I felt ashamed that I had only agreed to do it for the money.

"I hope you didn't find it too trying," the professor said, as he was driving me back to campus. "Not the world's most scintillating conversationalist, my mother."

"Oh, but I really liked her," I said. "She seems much more tranquil than Americans . . . at least the ones I know. Just contented with what *is*, not always thinking about wanting something else. What she's going to buy. It was very restful somehow."

He laughed. "There's nothing Zen about it, it's to do with a long history of deprivation. The old working-class mentality, make and mend all the way."

In fact, he told me, he was working on a book about the consumer culture in America, the emergence of shopping as a replacement for churchgoing, in pursuit of spiritual fulfillment. "And of course consumer capitalism can only perpetuate itself successfully if people are left permanently unsatisfied; at the point at which they're sated, they stop shopping, and the whole system falls apart. My mother's generation grew up poor, got married just before the war, and then lived with rationing for ten years. There was very little choice to be had. Hence they ceased to want. Whereas in America there's always been at least the illusion of choice."

Now all England was aflame with choice, or the illusion of it, the air was abuzz with people wanting things. I had only to get on the Tube or the 29 bus to be surrounded by young women with glossy shopping bags and artificial nails, chattering about what they'd just bought or were dying to buy or were about to exchange for something else. On my rare ventures to Oxford Street, where harsh blasts of rock music assaulted me even on the pavement, I was taken aback by how coiffed, how manicured, many of the women looked, and the nervous avidity in their faces. Reviews of themed gastropubs, flashy cars, different brands of truffle oil filled the Sunday supplements, alongside articles about architects building the City's new towers and financial whiz kids with gleaming American teeth. Even I kept receiving fliers about throat creams and tanning systems through the letter box, along with offers of credit cards on generous terms.

My landlord, entering into the spirit of things, painted the front door scarlet, wallpapered the downstairs hall, and raised my rent from £13.50 to £16.75 a week. It was then, when I had just spent the last of the John Deere money and panic was setting in—alien that I was, I could not apply for regular employment—that I stumbled into a freelance gig almost as implausible as the fantasies of my library friends. First came an article on Coronation souvenirs, for which I was paid handsomely, then one about the founder of the Battersea Dogs Home. No newsagent I came across ever carried the magazine in which these pieces appeared. Later I realized it was run largely for the benefit of its writers, many of whom seemed to be indigent poets.

I doubt that its American proprietor had ever read it himself. He had come to London at the tail end of a European tour, meaning to leave after a week. But one night in a pub near Cambridge Circus he fell into conversation with the publisher of a magazine named *London Calling*, about to be shut down due to impending bankruptcy. By the time last orders were called he had decided to buy it, and to stay on.

Two years earlier, his only son had died, aged eighteen, in a motorcycle crash on I-90, just outside Buffalo; his marriage had collapsed under the weight of that disaster, and after their separation his wife had moved to Manitoba, where she was born, to live with her brother. Meanwhile the money was piling in from the shopping malls he had built throughout Erie

County. And though his reading, as an adult, seemed largely confined to the tabloids, he had an exaggerated reverence for writers and writing: it seemed his immigrant grandfather used to read Dante aloud to him when he was a child. He would hand out wads of notes and tell his "boys"—I was one of just two female writers—to come up with something quaint to write about. That was pretty much the sum total of his instructions. And so there were articles about jousting tournaments, famous murders in Elizabethan London, the Chelsea Physic Garden, with here and there a little vignette about half-forgotten writers like Francis Thompson or Julian Maclaren-Ross, though he always insisted he didn't want to go too highbrow, the magazine was intended for a general audience, however mythical.

He was large, rumpled, gloomy, with a booming voice and a Brooklyn accent left over from childhood; sometimes, in his office on the Strand, still filled with the debris (old newspapers, old issues of the magazine, files stuffed with lawyers' letters) of his predecessor, he could be heard shouting at his minions back in Buffalo, always with reference to excrement. "Don't bullshit me, Danny"..."Don't give me that shit, Barreca"..."You gotta be shittin' me." But to us, his writers, he was the soul of courtesy. Whenever I entered, he would rise from his desk and remain standing until I was seated in the sagging armchair opposite, offer me whiskey even if it was ten in the morning, and ask hoarsely if I was okay for money.

"Tell me the truth, now. Do you get enough to eat?"
I got the feeling that if I said no he might start to cry.

Shortly after he took me on, he got the idea of distributing the magazine to hotels and B and Bs for free, which meant restaurants and pubs and even Madame Tussaud's gradually started placing ads, so he could pay his contributors with someone else's money. Once my philosopher friend saw someone reading it on the Tube. Mr. Cassini hired an advertising manager, whom nobody ever met, and installed him in an office somewhere in Hackney; he bought a new armchair, in red-and-green plaid, for his own office, and had the windows cleaned, though the debris remained.

Among the writers, his seeming favorite was a poet named Hugh, an old Etonian who dressed like a relic of the Mauve Decade, in a worn velvet jacket and a cravat, but for some inexplicable reason affected an Australian accent. His poems, which I'd occasionally seen in the *London Magazine*, were baroque in the extreme, with such knotty threads of allusion I rarely got through them, but he called Mr. Cassini "mate" and swilled bottles of ale in his office while they argued about Margaret Thatcher, whom Mr. Cassini admired extravagantly. One day, though, as I sat in the hall waiting to collect a check, I heard Hugh recite the whole of "Ode to a Nightingale" in pure Etonian English and then, at Mr. Cassini's urging, say it again, almost singing it this time. I remembered the first time I'd heard it, lying in bed in the dark, the tremor in my father's voice as he spoke the words. I went on listening as Hugh told Mr. Cassini what my father had told me that night, the story of illness and benighted love and early death, and "Here lies One Whose Name was writ in Water." "I can't stand it," Mr. Cassini growled, "oh, Jesus, you're killing me," and when Hugh had left, and I went in to get my money, his eyes were damp, he was blowing his nose on a large checked handkerchief he drew from his breast pocket.

Twelve

She said she wasn't trying to kill herself, she only
needed to let the pain out. Like a gas leak, she
said." Sasha again, except this time it felt real. A razor
slicing through flesh, the blood oozing out slowly and
then speeding up, that was scary. And something in
Isabel's voice, harsher than I'd ever heard it. Biting
back rage. I couldn't understand why she was suddenly
so angry at Sasha, especially now, until the story came
out and I realized it wasn't Sasha she was angry with.

Two subjects she'd never brought up with me till
then, whether from delicacy or embarrassment I wasn't
sure: one was Julian (in fact I sometimes wished she
would, I was curious, in a ghoulish way, but couldn't
bring myself to ask), the other was money. Of course
I knew she had some—enough not to worry—but in my
fantasy of her, she never gave it a thought, it didn't
enter into her scheme of things.

She must just have gotten back from Sasha's when I
phoned to remind her to bring a book I wanted to bor-
row to the Reading Room the next day. She sounded
frantic, telling me about the gouges in Sasha's arms.
Then she said, "This always happens when she gets

one of those letters." What letters? I asked, and after a silence that went on until I thought we'd been disconnected the story came pouring out, a whole Victorian novel condensed into a quarter hour.

Six years before, the lawyers had advised Helena to transfer the assets in her estate, after which she only had to live seven more years to avoid death duties altogether. And so she had put Sidworth in Julian's name. Everything but the house and the orchard that were Isabel's "patch" would go to him on her death, on condition that Helena be allowed to occupy the Hall undisturbed until she died.

"It's a bit of a joke, isn't it," Isabel said, "such a staunch feminist reverting to all those ancient notions of primogeniture. Perhaps down to genes after all. Of course a lot of people do that, but then they haven't just told their sons that their father wasn't who he thought he was. It seems a bit foolish of Mother not to have taken that into account." Secretly I felt offended that Julian had never told me about inheriting Sidworth; had he seen me as a gold digger, on top of all my other sins?

Anyway, after the final papers had been signed, when they were all at Sidworth for Christmas, Helena and Julian had their worst fight yet. He called her a monster, a praying mantis; she told him he was an utter mediocrity, a disappointment from birth, he'd inherited nothing from either parent. That same night he packed his bags and left, and ever after refused all contact: her letters came back unopened, her phone calls went unreturned. A few months later he left for Kenya.

Shortly after his return to England Helena had a stroke. When Isabel went to see her in the hospital she pleaded with her to effect a reconciliation. "She lay there moaning, she kept saying, 'My only son, my only son...I can't die until I see him again.' Over and over. It frightened me, I'd never seen her like that, I'd never seen her cry before. Not even for Maddy. Certainly not when my father died. But there she was, weeping, saying how sorry she was, how I must tell Julian she was sorry, she hadn't meant what she'd said. Another thing I'd never seen before. She was never sorry about anything.

"The next day I went up to London to see him. I told him she wasn't the same person we'd known as children, she was frail and old and sad, and she really loved him. I said how he and I were grown now, we were the ones with the power, not Mother, and wouldn't he rather use it better than she had? If he couldn't love her, at least he could forgive her, and that was all she was asking, really, she wouldn't expect anything more."

"I don't think this story is going to end well."

"No." She was silent for a moment. "He said to spare him the *East Lynne* rubbish." I could imagine that so well. "But I still went on trying. That first night I met you, I was there to ask him again."

("Nothing much," he'd said, when I asked him what she'd wanted to talk to him about.)

"Though by that time she was much better. The doctors had said she'd never walk again, but she proved them wrong. Much to her delight. And the stronger she got, the less humble she was. Until finally she was her old self again, and since then it's been all-out war. She threatened to kill herself exactly one day before the seven years was up, so he'd have to pay the death duties after all. That was part of the reason she took those sleeping tablets last November, she was practicing.

"She started consulting lawyers, they told her she couldn't alter the trust but there was a legal distinction between her personal estate and the 'furnishings and fixtures' at Sidworth, which had to go to him. Her personal effects she could dispose of as she wanted. So she had a codicil drawn up, leaving certain things to Sasha and me, and she started selling things off, to put more money in trust for Sasha. Unfortunately, someone alerted Julian to the presence of the little Renoir in a Christie's catalogue, and after that he made sure his lawyers monitored the auction houses. But some of the furious letters flying back and forth are about objects that aren't actually worth very much. Probably less than the lawyers charge for writing them. Like the Kelmscott Press edition of *Utopia*, which Mother is leaving to me. She says she bought it herself—I don't know if that's true—and Julian says it was Grandfather's. She says the St. Nicholas icon Grandmother brought from St. Petersburg as a bride was Grandmother's twenty-first birthday present to her. With

Julian insisting they're part of his inheritance. And so it goes on."

It seemed both Isabel and Sasha were routinely enlisted to buttress one or the other's claims. The latest object of contention was a Corot drawing of women reapers, which Helena maintained was a gift to her from Roger, and Julian claimed had belonged to his grandfather. Julian wanted Sasha to sign an affidavit saying it had hung in the study for as long as she could remember. "Which is completely meaningless, since Mother says Roger gave it to her in 1958, when Sasha was all of four. I told her I'd point that out to Julian, but she wouldn't let me. Instead she went into a funk and sliced her wrists. She'll do anything rather than say no to him outright. Because she's the only one on his side, she says, he doesn't have anybody else. It must be a sort of hangover from childhood... She worshipped him when she was young, though he could be really beastly to her, he wasn't exactly the ideal brother. But she goes into a rage if I mention that. She says I never really loved him, not the way she does... and then she says it about herself, she's just an object of charity to me, by that time she's shouting, I don't love her the way Lucy does, Lucy is the only one who *really* loves her. You see what a mess it is. Maybe I ought to ask Lucy to talk to her about the Corot, she might listen if Lucy said it."

"But would Lucy do that?"

"Oh God, yes, she'll do anything for Sasha. She always would. Even when she was very young, and Sasha was in hospital, she never seemed to find her peculiar.

I suppose most adult behavior was mystifying to her anyway, Sasha's no more than other people's; those odd jumps she made, from one subject to another, they never made Lucy uncomfortable the way they did everyone else. She was pleased as anything when Sasha had a phase of only talking in rhyme, she did her best to keep up. And Sasha was good with her too, at least at times; she let Lucy order her around when she was in her bossy stage. 'Come along, Aunt Sasha,' she'd say, in the voice of her teacher from infants' school, 'time for a walk. The fresh air will do you good.' And Sasha would walk out in the grounds with her, holding hands, though she never would with me.

"Even when Sasha was surly with her, and barely spoke, or crumpled up a drawing Lucy made for her and threw it away, she never held it against her. Once she explained to me, after Sasha had been particularly horrid, that Sasha must have had the roar in her head that day. Sasha had told her on one of their walks about the roar; it was like an ocean sometimes, she said, and sometimes like the buzzing of bees. 'It must be dreadful, Mummy, don't you think?' Yes, I said, terrible, though I hated Sasha that day.

"Poor Lucy—I didn't give her much of a family, did I? No one besides a mad aunt to love. No father, no sisters or brothers, a grandmother who hardly took any notice of her. And of course Julian was useless. Which is why I started going back to Patras with her, after the junta fell." Stavros's sisters and aunts and cousins made a huge fuss of Lucy, she said, converging on his mother's narrow gray house on the outskirts of the city to cook enormous meals, the adults vying with each other to tell her stories of her father's childhood, the children teaching her to say "shit" and "ass" in Greek, which they thought was the funniest thing ever.

Isabel had been forgiven, it seems, for bringing Lucy into the world without the benefit of marriage. "Mostly his mother let the others speak, she just sat in her chair next to the stove and listened. It was because her English wasn't good enough, she said. But she followed closely, nodding in agreement, or breaking in to correct them in her heavy accent—not so, Stavros wasn't yet thirteen when the nose of him was broken in the football, he was twelve only. Unlike his sisters, she never cried over those reminiscences; she would gesture to her daughters to blow their noses, wipe their faces, heaving herself up to fetch a cloth for the purpose. Sometimes it unnerved me a little, the way she watched Lucy so closely as they spoke, as though she was gauging her reactions, sizing her up. And when we left to go back to England, she'd just kiss her once, on her forehead, she wouldn't hug her the way the others did. But then she'd grip her hand and say two things to her in Greek: 'Good-bye, my beloved, be a good girl, come back to us soon.' And '*Na thymasai panta, imaste i oikogeneia sou.*' Always remember, we are your family. Which I think she always did."

She broke off. "But this is unconscionable of me . . . I've been wittering on at you about my family for hours. You must be bored to tears."

"Don't be crazy. I haven't been bored for a second. Is Sasha okay now, though? Did you have to take her to the hospital?"

But it seemed Sasha hadn't needed first aid; years of practice with razors and Swiss army knives and scissors, long experience in slicing off thin ribbons of flesh, had taught her exactly how deep to go, where the arteries were that had to be circumvented. She could create pretty patterns, even, crisscrossing lines and delicate sworls between the wrist and the inside of the elbow. Only iodine and bandages had been needed. Daphne—Tuesdays were Daphne's days off; Sasha had timed her self-mutilation in the hours between her leaving and Isabel's arrival—promised to check the post in future and send any solicitors' letters to Isabel. As for the Corot drawing: in the end it turned out it wasn't a Corot after all, it was an early twentieth-century forgery, so that problem was solved.

Part Three

Thirteen

Two days before I left for America, meaning never to return, my friends from the Reading Room insisted on giving me a farewell lunch I knew they couldn't afford. Their cardigans were shabbier than ever, their teeth more stained, but their jokes were as erudite as always, their eyes bright and hot, hungry for fun. Except now I couldn't deal with it. They were forcing me to pretend, for a full two hours, that life was a droll and merry affair; if they were only pretending too, that no longer struck me as touching gallantry. I would have preferred for us to sit there exchanging harsh truths.

They toasted my new life with glasses of Australian wine; they presented me with a Victorian copy of the *Biographia Literaria* as a parting gift, in pretty silver wrapping, with a white bow. Guilt-stricken, unworthy, I went round the table, kissing each of them in turn. I rolled my eyes as I told them about Hiawatha and the world's largest shopping mall and the average annual snowfall in the Twin Cities.

But all the time I was thinking of the inquest, remembering the stuffy smell in the room, sweat overlaid with Dettol, and the hard, worn benches and the clearing of throats. The judge had offered his solemn condolences to Isabel's mother, who bowed her head majestically, in silent acknowledgment. When I called Alexei afterward he told me he couldn't talk just then and hung up.

On the face of it, Isabel and Alexei were the most unlikely pair imaginable, you could hardly even picture them in the same room. But maybe nobody since Stavros had breached her defenses with such blithe disregard. Or been on such a mission to save the world.

It was through Mr. Cassini, whose passion for lost causes was seemingly inexhaustible, that I'd hooked up with him. On one of his pub crawls Mr. Cassini had met a man from the Royal Society who told him about Alexei: an intellectual shaman, he called him, obsessed with some Russian mathematicians he claimed had broken the logjam in set theory back in the days of the czars; some of them had been monks, and their theory of functions was actually based on an ancient mystical tradition, condemned by first the Orthodox Church and then the Communists. Through heroic effort, this wild man had managed to track down their papers and private journals, smuggled out of Russia during the Stalinist era. At the very least, the guy in the pub said, it was a great story.

Mr. Cassini tracked Alexei down at his shabby office over a kebab shop in Oxford; he had a small grant from the university's mathematics faculty to oversee the publication of the papers, but his deadline had come and gone, the money was running out, and nobody was willing to provide more funding. It was shameful, he said on the phone, a disgrace, inimical to mankind's best interests: the ramifications of the Name Worshippers' work went far beyond mathematics; it constituted nothing less than an alternative to Western materialism.

Mr. Cassini sent him a check for a thousand pounds, but could do no more, his resources having been stretched to the limit. The profits from his Buffalo investments had nose-dived in his absence. He suspected Mr. Barreca of skimming off the profits, and was about to fly back to take control of his empire himself. But before he left he formulated a strategy to address Alexei's plight: get him "fabulous" publicity in America, generate excitement; then the Rockefeller or Ford Foundation could be persuaded to fund his project. I, being an American, was his chosen instrument for this plan; I was supposed to publish an article in an American magazine, explaining the dramatic implications of Alexei's work for the regeneration of society.

I pointed out that I knew less than nothing about math, and anyway *Art & Antiques* wasn't likely to run a story on set theory. "But this guy wants to save humanity. You know that, right? And what if he could, just a little bit? What if he could make this messed-up old world just a teeny bit better, bring it half an inch closer to what God wants for us? Don't we have to help him? Come on. You're saying you won't even go hear what he's got to say? And write a few crummy letters to some magazines? I can't believe I'm hearing this."

So I caved in and took a train to Oxford, where Alexei, peering at me over little gold glasses, running his hands excitably through his mane of white hair—he looked a bit like Einstein, which made it easier to suspend disbelief—delivered himself of an impassioned speech about Cantor's beautiful spirit and the different types of infinity. He kept rummaging through the battered metal shelves to find yet another notebook or yellowed sheet of paper that he insisted I look at, never mind that, when they didn't consist wholly of numbers, they were in Russian, which I had to keep reminding him I didn't understand. "I will translate for you," he said, although when he did, my comprehension didn't extend much further.

"But this is absurd, to try to write all I say in a notebook, this is not the proper way to interview someone," he said, clutching his head in distress, and dug out a tape recorder from the debris beneath his desk. We agreed that I would return it to him when I had finished transcribing the tapes, and meet again then to discuss the article further, in London this time. It was then I had the idea of bringing Isabel. I remembered her saying how she'd fallen in love with maths as an adolescent, only Sasha was so much better that she realized she didn't have a real gift. Still, she'd done maths at A-level, which put her way ahead of me.

She'd know the right questions to ask, she could tell me if his fixation on those monks was warranted or just plain nuts. If I thought at all about how she'd see him, I assumed it would be how I did: as an exotic throwback, a figure from a nineteenth-century Russian novel.

It was two years since our first meeting in the Reading Room. A few months before, I'd met a man at a *TLS* party, a thirty-six-year-old lecturer in history at Birkbeck, and embarked on a relationship that felt so uncomplicatedly easy I sometimes forgot his existence for hours at a time. I never once retreated to the ladies' room of a restaurant where we were eating to gaze at myself anxiously in the mirror, hoping I hadn't veered into hideousness during the course of the entrée. "Would you call this a love affair?" I asked him one night, as we lay in bed in his flat in Tufnell Park, his hand resting on my thigh, and he said, "Let's just say we have a taste for each other's company."

His name was Jack; a miner's son from Durham, he was now a member of what he called the North London chattering classes, mostly consisting of academics and journalists and a few therapists—a profession Jack regarded as a load of bollocks. Nobody in Durham, apparently, had ever paid good money to have someone listen to him whine about his problems. Another thing he was derisive about, with many cheerful snorts, was my romance with his "fucked-up, feudal" country. He claimed to prefer Americans for their openness, their bracing directness, though one of the most endearing things he ever told me was that the first time he'd gone to Manhattan, flying Laker's Skytrain when he was just out of university, he really believed that if he offended a New Yorker—jostled a man in the subway, ordered a jelly doughnut in a coffee shop that had run out of jelly doughnuts—whoever it was might take out a gun and shoot him. Of course he laughed as he said it, but when we flew together to New York during his spring break I noticed he was wholly unlike his usual combative self. Even when my brother, who had come from Pittsburgh to see us, was telling him about the revolutionary potential of thrash metal music, even when Joannie's husband described spending the night on the gym floor with his students, with only newspapers for blankets, to give them insight into the experience of homelessness, he only nodded at intervals and made murmurous *hmmmm* noises vaguely indicative of assent. It made me wonder if the thought of that gun was still lurking somewhere.

I'd been scared that the whole city would seem haunted, I'd be flooded with guilt or nostalgia or both, but only very rarely—turning the corner onto Second Avenue, the wind blowing bits of paper and grit into my face, or catching sight of a sign for Long Island City—did it feel as though Eliot was somewhere still, for a snatch of a minute the reality of him became so vivid that it knocked me off balance. Which happened sometimes in England too, when I was just on the brink of sleep. But mostly I had a slightly skittish sense of disconnection the whole time we were in New York, as though I weren't quite present; my body had been transported from England but I hadn't arrived yet.

Only in Gurneyville, my mother in her familiar green armchair, in her familiar green housecoat, did I feel wholly real to myself, back in touch with my past—all the old guilt and pity and anger and resentment, the waters closing over my head.

As far as the conversation went, I might have been visiting from Poughkeepsie, or Chittenango. The first thing she did when I arrived was to tell me that the TV was on the blink. "That's not my fault," I snapped, though she hadn't said it was—it was only that all her complaints were uttered in a tone of reproach, so that even when she told me, via long distance, that Mrs. Zincke had fallen and broken her hip, she wouldn't be coming by with hot meals for a while, I felt as though somehow this too was my fault, or at least I should fill in for her, I should be providing those hot meals.

"I don't suppose you could take a look at it," she said mournfully. And because she clearly had no real hope that I'd fix it, I was determined to. I fiddled with the knobs, I checked all the wires at the back to make sure they weren't loose, and then removed them and blew into the holes, in case dust was the problem. When none of that worked, I thumped it on its side. "Stop that," my mother said sharply, "you're hurting it"—as though the television were the sentient object, not me. "Go on, get away from there." Those little eruptions, when she awakened from her habitual daze, were always startling; in those years after my father left my brother and I would ignore her for hours or days, fix our own meals, shovel the path, squabble with each other over whose turn it was to do the dishes, and then suddenly, without warning, she'd rouse herself, she might attack with a dish towel, or her nails, or just stand up and shriek that she wished we'd never been born. Though she'd slump back into her chair a minute later, as though nothing had happened, we were always a little leery of her for a while afterward.

She hardly looked at the presents I had brought her, all those guilt offerings from London: a Royal Doulton cup and saucer, Yardley talcum powder, a paisley scarf. "Why don't you wear it now?" I said brightly, but she shook her head. "Those new pills for my heart aren't doing a darn bit of good." After that we sat in silence for a minute, until, hysteria mounting, I leapt to my feet. "You know what? I think we should rearrange the furniture. Wouldn't that be fun? Wouldn't you be glad of a change?" And when she didn't outright refuse, I started jerking the couch across the room, pushing first one side and then another, huffing and puffing, till it stood in the opposite corner. I dragged the coffee table across the carpet, picked up the side table with the lamp and stuck it next to the couch, moved everything but the chair she was sitting on, exclaiming in false delight as I stood back and examined my work. "There! Isn't that better? It makes the room seem more spacious, don't you think?"

She looked me in the face then, pityingly, as though sensing my desperation; she gave a little sigh and leaned toward me, her lips parted. It flashed into my head that she was going to say I couldn't change her life by changing the furniture around. I knew there was no answer to that, I dreaded hearing her say it, but I almost wanted her to, at least there'd be some kind of truth between us. Instead she fell back again. "If you say so." After that there was more about Mrs. Zincke, and the pills, and the new social worker, a big fat lady, not half as pretty as the girl that used to come. The very last thing she said, as I was leaving to catch the bus back to the city, was about the TV: "I bet Eliot could have fixed it," she said. "Eliot was so good at fixing things."

Fourteen

Alexei had suggested we meet at a Lebanese restaurant near Paddington, a special place, according to him, "extremely delightful." Actually it looked
vaguely like a brothel, with red brocade wallpaper
and dirty fringed tablecloths and a single, menacing-
looking waiter who kept disappearing behind a bead
curtain, shouting in an unidentifiable language at
someone we couldn't see. But Alexei ushered me to a
table with an air of satisfaction and sat looking expectantly at the door until Isabel arrived. "So," he said,
rising, clasping her hand, "so this is the lady mathematician!" He ignored her demurrals and gestured at the
waiter. "I think this calls for some wine, no?"

"What a very nice idea," Isabel said politely, though
she and I usually stuck to coffee at our lunches. Alexei
spent a few minutes pondering the wine list, as the two
of us made slightly awkward conversation, and then
snapped it shut decisively and ordered. "One bottle
to begin with, yes?" Oh, yes, we said, that would definitely be enough.

He leaned across the table toward her. "I have heard
that now the English are having their own vineyards,

they want to be wine producers. Poor them." He shook his head. "I am afraid they will make a sad muck of it, as you say."

"Well, Russia is hardly a wine-making country either," I pointed out, and he raised a finger.

"There you are very wrong. There are some fine wines coming out of the Caucasus, quite excellent pinot noirs. But then they know what they are doing, they have been making wines in their villages for some time."

"How interesting," Isabel murmured, and she did seem interested, not perhaps in the question of wine production in Russia, but in the oddness of him. A moment later, when she asked about his work, and he was telling her how the Russians had built on Cantor's work on infinities, had dared to consider its metaphysical implications, which the French, brainwashed by Descartes, had strenuously resisted, she asked him politely if he was referring to antinomies. The waiter had just set the wineglasses down, and was opening the bottle. Alexei ignored the glass the man was proffering for him to taste.

"You see?" he said accusingly. "You too have been brainwashed. This nonsense about antinomies is only an evasion of Cantor's formulation of the Absolute, which even the Germans tried to ignore as if it was a bad smell." He screwed up his face in a pantomime of disgust to illustrate the point. "For that reason it is vital that the works of the Russians be properly explicated, so that people will be returned to a spiritual understanding of the subject."

"Sir," the waiter said.

Alexei gulped back the half inch of wine in the glass and grimaced. "Never mind. It is good enough for us. We are not such connoisseurs." He leaned across to Isabel again. "I sincerely hope that you will come to Oxford and see the papers for yourself. There is so much I would like to show you. And perhaps you will even write something for a mathematical journal." He beamed. "I have thought that ever since I heard you were coming today. I have you much in my sights."

"But that's out of the question. Truly. There's no chance I'll even understand what they're talking about."

"I will help you to understand. And if it comes from an Englishwoman, from a graduate of your great Cambridge, then people will be more likely to believe it. They will see these are not just old monks with long beards. Surely you won't refuse at least to come and look."

She would be very interested to see the papers sometime, she said weakly, but he mustn't think she could ever write about them.

"Excellent! Then we shall drink to your visit!" As he held his glass aloft, I thought for a moment he was going to drain it in one go and smash it against the wall. When he was not discoursing learnedly on the limits of Cartesian mathematics, it was easy to imagine him breaking into a Cossack dance. He even looked like a Cossack, with his broad face, his thick, untidy white hair and luxuriant mustache.

But he behaved himself, and the lunch progressed smoothly. Julian should have seen Isabel then, with her cheeks flushed and wisps of hair falling out of its knot onto her face. Alexei was looking at her with frank admiration; he poured her more wine, over her protests, not noticing that my glass was empty too, and roared with laughter when her napkin fell off her lap, and they both leaned down to pick it up, and their heads bumped.

"How did you come to be so interested in the Name Worshippers?" she asked him. "Did they teach their work in Russia?"

Of course he had not heard of them in Russia, he said, certainly not, they had been banned by the state, and then he launched into a story he had told me, in much less detail, in Oxford. His mother, a lab technician (his father had been killed in the last year of the war; he had never known him), had been transferred to work in an industrial lab in Magdeburg, in East Germany, when he was sixteen. In Smolensk, he had been regarded as the most promising mathematician in his school; he had placed second in a national competition during his last year there. But in the East German school he had made the mistake of pointing out the mistakes of his math teacher—an idiot, he said, with the soul of a petty bureaucrat and a brother high up in the Party. And so he had been expelled for "antisocial attitudes," "unhealthy individualism," and assigned to work in a coal mine near Leipzig, where it was hoped he could learn a more communitarian spirit.

He had three days before he had to report to his new employment. On the second day he decided that, rather than make the journey to Leipzig, he would try to slip over the border. His mother added bread and wurst and a flask of coffee to the identity cards and clean underwear in his rucksack, and as soon as it was dark he got on his bicycle and headed for the Elbe. In the end, he'd had to abandon the bicycle and cross to the west by clinging to the bottom of a barge. The very next day, having presented himself to the proper West German authorities, he was assigned a guardian (he was, after all, a minor), who turned out to be a former SS man. "Imagine that!" he said, laughing uproariously. "I had escaped to truth and freedom, and this noble democracy placed me in the care of a Nazi."

That laugh of his, so boisterous and yet so devoid of mirth, reddening his face with what could have been anger, unnerved me, but on Isabel it seemed to have a different effect. Her face softened; she appeared more moved by his laughter than by the story of leaving his mother behind and taking off in the dark. I had noticed before that she wasn't always sympathetic to accounts of physical deprivation; maybe they embarrassed her, she took them as implying a reproach to herself. But a person mocking the absurdity of his illusions: that was something she could understand, and feel pity for.

Anyway, he said, the old Nazi made his living, and a good one, by taking in teenaged boys sent to him by the state: Alexei's fellow orphans included a fourteen-year-old Swabian flower grower's son whose parents had been killed in a car crash and two scared little thugs whose mothers had vanished without a trace. The Nazi fed them on gruel and cheese rinds and day-old black bread the baker sold at a discount, though he received a generous allowance from the state. Alexei was as hungry in his first few weeks there, he said, as he had been in Russia during the war.

Soon he was apprenticed to a tool-and-die maker—the best education he'd ever had, he claimed, the only one of value to him in his present task, since it taught him the importance of close attention. But meanwhile he was studying at night, first German, which he'd hardly had time to learn properly in Leipzig, and then calculus. By the time he was eighteen, and legally free of the Nazi's guardianship, he was ready to sit the entrance exams for the university. After obtaining his baccalaureate in mathematics, he went on to graduate school in Berlin, to work toward his Ph.D.

It was during his graduate studies in Berlin that he stumbled on the work of the Russian mathematicians, quite by accident. He had been feeling very despondent, he said; the work he was doing, on the fractal dimensions of Julia sets, had come to seem sterile to him. His mother had died a few months back, in Leipzig, without his ever seeing her again. He went round to the flat of a friend of his from the university, a woman whose name he had forgotten, though he did remember that she was wearing green stockings that day, which he'd never seen before. The friend with the green stockings—from the way he said it, it was clear she was not just a friend—was on the telephone when he arrived, so he started looking idly through a stack of journals on her desk for something to occupy himself with. In an article on Cantor sets, he saw a footnote referring to a group of Russian mystics who'd defied the determinism of their French and German counterparts and dared to use mathematics as a means of approaching the transcendent "One" of Plotinus.

With his eyes fixed on Isabel's face, he made a fist and held it solemnly to his breast. "Then a great illumination took place, an explosion in my brain. I went straight to the library to see what more I could find about those men, and when I learned that some of their papers, particularly those on the moral relevance of discontinuous functions, had been smuggled out of Russia at the time of the Stalinist purges, I knew I had found my calling. I swore to myself that I would track down those writings and bring them to light no matter how long it took."

I gave her a nervous glance, but there was no trace of mockery in her expression.

"It is not just mathematics and theology that they interested themselves in," he went on. "They felt and understood very much about culture, society, the position of women. You will be interested to read the journals of Ivanov, what he says of his wife, and of other women also. He had several mistresses, always remarkable women in their own right. And always he pays tribute to them as the true repositories of wisdom."

"Ah yes," she said dryly. "The famous wisdom of women. Everyone's so eager to give them credit for that, as long as they don't mistake it for power."

Alexei, however, was incapable of humor on the subject of his idols. "It is not this stupidity he is making, not at all. He is humbled by the spiritual greatness he perceives in these women, their closeness to nature. He saw how the men of his time were living increasingly out of harmony with nature, how they saw it only as something to conquer for their own ends. There are many entries foreseeing the environmental destruction that is ever increasing, he understood the need to be awakened to its dangers. And he believed that women could show the way. It is the heirs of the Enlightenment who distrusted women, who regarded them as inferior. Because to them reason was everything, and so in their narrowness of vision they scorned women for knowing nothing of the continuum theory and such matters. Now women too have absorbed the lessons of the Enlightenment, and what do they do? Ape the very worst qualities of the men. Behold your Mrs. Thatcher. She is the result of empowerment without the soul's wisdom behind it. She has no more spiritual greatness than the men who surround her."

"She's hardly *my* Mrs. Thatcher," Isabel said, but he waved this away.

"If you will come to the archive, I can show you passages that will astonish you. You will see that these men showed a way out of the soulless materialism of our time, they have cleared a path for a transformation of our society. People only have to hear what they have to say, they must be made to understand." He looked at her sternly, as though recalling her to a moral duty she had neglected for too long, yet his whole manner, the way his eyes were fixed so urgently on hers, was a kind of erotic pleading. She, meanwhile, was looking helplessly back at him; I couldn't tell if she was falling under his spell or merely feeling trapped. "Besides," he said, as though it were the clinching argument, "you have Russian blood, you will understand those things in them that so frighten the English as well as the others." Only later did it occur to me to wonder how he'd known that she had Russian blood, or, for that matter, that she'd gone to Cambridge; there was no Google in those days, no Internet, it took a certain amount of effort to discover such things about people.

When the waiter came with the bill, Alexei took it from him, looked it over, nodding to himself, and then announced cheerfully that he was afraid we would have to pay his share; he was completely out of cash, he said, and his credit card was back at the office. "I keep it in a drawer, you see, and then I forget to take it with me. Very stupid. But when you come to the archive"— he was addressing Isabel, of course—"I will take you for a beautiful meal, to atone."

I was a little annoyed, as the bill for a very indifferent meal came to almost a hundred pounds—he had ordered a second bottle of wine, which he'd mostly drunk himself—and I was pretty broke myself at that point, but Isabel only said, "Never mind," in that austerely polite tone she always used when the subject of money arose, as though to fend off any further discussion. And so we split the bill between the two of us.

As the waiter counted the notes we'd handed over, his eyes narrowed with concentration or suspicion or both, Alexei looked at his watch and exclaimed at the time. He really must leave, he said, a Greek mathematician, a Dr. Sotiropoulos, was coming to his office that afternoon, to discuss the Russians; he would already be late. "But first we must make our plans." He leaned toward her. "Tell me when you will come." His voice was hoarse, and hers was not quite steady when she said she didn't know, she would have to look at her calendar.

"But you will definitely come," he said.

I stood up abruptly, feeling like a voyeur. "I've got to go myself, I have a review to write for the *TLS*."

"Lovely to see you," Isabel said. "We must meet again soon." It was plain she hardly knew what her mouth was saying, her brain was utterly disengaged. Her face, normally so pale, was a rosy pink; for a moment I wondered if she was wearing a new kind of blush. I gave her a kiss on the cheek and went to shake Alexei's hand, but he leapt up and enveloped me in a bear hug, squeezing me until I was breathless.

"Wonderful," he said, "wonderful." I'm not sure he knew himself what he was referring to. I don't believe either of them was thinking straight at that point.

Because despite what happened later, despite how Isabel came to see it, I'm ready to swear he wasn't just acting that day, it wasn't all part of a calculated plan. I saw how he looked at her, I heard the catch in his voice.

Still, the fact remains that he'd come to that lunch knowing who she was, and by that I mean not the author of a fine, respected book on the religious origins of dance, but the daughter of a famous mother, with connections to people who wielded power in various circles. However careful Isabel was to keep the information off her book jacket—she bore her father's unremarkable surname—the gossips of the academic world would have talked.

Maybe Alexei thought of the English establishment as akin to the Politburo, or the KGB, only with better tailors at their disposal: a shadowy cabal determining people's fates in secret. Helena Denby had a cousin in the House of Lords, she was interviewed on the radio, the Prince of Wales had expressed admiration for her stance on pesticides. Alexei probably believed she had only to endorse him for his funding to be restored. He must have hoped that at a word from her, they would reinstate his grant, perhaps Bernard Williams would write the introduction to his book. Even now, it's easier for me than it would have been for Isabel to imagine what it felt like to be Alexei, forty-seven and desperate, staring ruin in the face.

Mr. Cassini might have saved him, but he never returned from Buffalo. He died there, of a heart attack, in a rented hotel room not far from where his son had been killed. Mr. Barreca, whom he'd shouted at so often down the phone, came to London a few weeks later and canceled the printer's order for the magazine's next issue. Within a few days he'd sold the lease on the premises to a hops trader and shut us all down.

Fifteen

Back from lunch in a grumpy mood, I found a message taped to my door: "Phone Jack. Urgent." But when I did, he wouldn't tell me what it was about. "Get over here. I'll explain when I see you."

"Oh, come on. Tell me. I just got back, I don't feel like dragging myself out again."

"Just come," he said maddeningly.

"That's the kind of thing you accuse women of. Acting all secretive and making men beg them to say what it is."

But he had hung up.

On my arrival, he took me by the hand without a word and led me into the kitchen, where he seated me, still in my coat, at the table. Then he paced back and forth, still without speaking, as though the news were too important to come out with right away. Finally, just as I was thinking brain tumor, he told me: he had gotten a phone call from Gareth, a chum from his graduate-school days at York, who was now teaching medieval history at the University of Minnesota. Their nineteenth- and twentieth-century British guy had been diagnosed with pancreatic cancer, they were looking for someone to take over his classes after the spring break, Gareth had suggested Jack. They wanted him to fly out immediately for an interview that, according to Gareth, was mostly a formality: they had twenty-four days to find someone, they'd seemed more than happy to take his word for Jack's brilliance. The salary on offer was three times what he was earning at Birkbeck, where his contract was strictly term to term, but even if things didn't pan out, he had nothing to lose by going: they would pay his fare and all his expenses. "At the very least, I'll get to see the Mississippi River."

I had never seen him so keyed up: back and forth, back and forth he went in the narrow space between the table and the fridge, holding a cracked white mug of what could have been tea but might have been whiskey. He was barefoot, I kept thinking he was going to catch cold from the icy lino. Finally he stopped and turned to me. "So what do you think?"

"I suppose you ought to go," I said in a carefully neutral voice, trying to suppress the selfish thought that this would be the end of us. "Like you said, there's nothing to lose."

He came and put his mug down, looming over me. "Of course I'm going to go. What I mean is, if they offer me the job, will you come with me?"

We had never talked about the future, never made loverlike vows about forever, or even next year. I felt like a character in a Victorian novel: I am sensible of the great honor you are conferring on me, but . . .

"Why don't we wait and see what happens? There's no point in making plans yet."

"But don't you see what this means? We could actually live off my salary, you could write a real book instead of all that crap journalism."

The only thing I wanted at that moment was for him to stop hanging over me; instead he kept looking at me expectantly, he seemed to be waiting for me to shout Hallelujah, to throw my arms around him. But all I could muster was a feeble "It's not all crap. I mean, some of it isn't so bad."

"Christ," he said, kicking the table leg. "I thought you'd be happy about this. I thought we'd be celebrating."

Of course I was happy for him, I said, it was great news, the best, but he couldn't expect me to make up my mind just like that. Then I added snidely that if he was worried about finding female companionship there would be plenty of impressionable young coeds he could seduce—referring to his previous girlfriend, one of his "mature" students at Birkbeck. Starting a fight was the only way I could think of to buy myself time.

"Sod off." He marched to the cupboard and poured a slug of whiskey into his mug without offering me any; then he stalked away, muttering under his breath.

I took off my coat, poured the scaly water out of the kettle, refilled it, and made myself a cup of tea that I carried into the front room, where he sat on the sagging couch. A rerun of a Parliamentary debate was playing on the black-and-white telly that was perched on a pile of gramophone records (the gramophone, in the opposite corner, was perched on a pile of books). I tried a more conciliatory tone. We had never even lived together, I pointed out reasonably; wasn't he worried that it might not work out? What if it turned out to be a mistake, and there we were, marooned in the middle of the American heartland together?

"Sod off," he said again, without turning his head.

I stormed over and switched off the television, almost toppling it in my righteous fury, and a kind of madness erupted. If I expected him to grovel, he yelled, if I wanted him to beg me on bended knee, then I'd chosen the wrong man. He was nothing but a coward, I shrieked, for all his bluster he was just afraid of everything beyond his cozy little London existence in this rotten flat, and by the way, why the hell didn't he clean it occasionally, did he think it showed his heroic defiance of bourgeois values to have a filthy toilet and cobwebs everywhere? Were those Lawrentian cobwebs? Anyway, it was bullshit to talk about the books I could write; it wasn't what I wanted that mattered, it was all about him, he was just afraid someone was going to shoot him when he got there. Maybe he should buy a gun, that would solve the problem.

Fine, he said, he'd go by himself, probably he'd be better off. At least he wouldn't have to put up with my bloody moods, and all those fucking little riffs I kept trotting out at parties. Did I know how sick he was of hearing about my adolescent fantasies of England, and the goddamn dying earl's model of the *Flying Scotsman*? (This was in reference to my most poignant assignment for *Art & Antiques*, when I'd traveled to Suffolk to report on a decrepit aristocrat's collection of antique model trains, housed in the one remaining tower of his crumbling stone castle.) And how fascinating did he suppose I found all *his* little riffs at this point, I asked, banging my mug down on the windowsill, so that milky tea sloshed over onto an ancient copy of the *New Statesman*. If I had to listen to him ranting one more time about the sinister implications of computers, or public school wankers, or the Lewis Carroll logic of English bureaucracy, I was going to slit my wrists. Not to mention his habit of asking me, in an accusatory voice, where his wallet had got to, or his clean socks. I didn't even live there, for Christ's sake, how should I know where his goddamn socks were? And now he expected me to throw up everything and follow him to the wilds of Minnesota, where presumably I could spend my days rearranging his sock drawer. What was I, the fucking handmaiden to his fucking genius?

I was still waiting for the coach to Brideshead, he said, toot toot, all aboard. Didn't he realize he was one of the chattering classes himself, I said: what did he think he was, a worker? With a Ph.D. from York? Give me a break. Anyway Karl Marx was a hypocritical shit, he made his bastard kid by the housekeeper use the servants' entrance. And Arthur Scargill was a vicious egomaniacal bully. If I thought Isabel was really my friend, he said (he had met her exactly once, he had said she had beautiful eyes, and pronounced her all right for one of them), I was deluding myself: she just wanted me as a lapdog. Professors who seduced their students were morally despicable, I yelled. And there was more, much more, the non sequiturs flying thick and fast.

Always before, our arguments had been mere sullen affairs, carried on via mutters or broody silences: "What's wrong?" "Nothing." "Come off it. Why don't you just tell me?" "Oh, leave me alone." That sort of thing. Now we had exploded into fury; there was something almost thrilling about it, in a sick kind of way, as though we'd ascended to a whole new level of passion.

At one point I really thought he was going to hit me; at another, I found myself jumping up and down like a lunatic on the threadbare Moroccan rug, screaming at him to get out. "What are you talking about?" he said mildly. "This is my flat, remember?" I had grabbed my coat, preparatory to storming out myself, when he took hold of my arm, not roughly but with just enough force to detain me. "Calm down, why don't you. Drink your tea."

"It's cold."

"I'll make you a fresh cup." And suddenly I was exhausted; I nodded meekly, put my coat on top of the television, and sat down at his desk. As quickly as it had erupted, it seemed, the fury had died away.

When he returned he was holding two chipped mugs without handles. He set one down in front of me. "At least if you get the job you can afford to buy some decent mugs," I said, trying for a joke. But I could not look at him. "When do they want you for this interview?"

"Right away. Next Wednesday."

"What about Birkbeck?"

"I'll have to cancel the Thursday seminar. But Bob Rigden will fill in for me the Tuesday after. And if I leave, they won't have any trouble filling my slot . . . I suppose if this comes through I'll have to get a car."

"Probably. Though they do have public transport, you know. It's a big city, it's not the Wild West."

"But Gareth's always talking about the blizzards. You wouldn't want to hang about at bus stops in that weather."

"You might not want to drive in it either. Especially on the other side of the road. And if you break down you can die of exposure. Every day on the news they announce the coldest place in the continental United States. And every day it's International Falls, Minnesota."

"And on that note of buoyant optimism . . . first it was my rotten character, now it's the weather. You're just scratching around for reasons not to go."

The Twin Cities were where we'd flown when we visited Eliot's parents in St. Cloud, but that wasn't it, not really; nor was it about our never having lived together. The thought of going back to America felt suffocating. It wasn't for all the reasons that made sense, like missing the Reading Room or Radio Four or the Heath or even Isabel, but because I'd no longer be a foreigner, I'd lose the freedom not to belong.

"The funny thing is, I can easily imagine you there, walking around campus with your battered satchel. Everyone saying, 'Oooh, I love your accent.' But it's different for me. People will expect me to be an American."

"So put on an English accent. I've heard you do it with strangers. 'Yes, quite,' you say, in a teddibly English voice."

"Then they'll ask me if I'm English, and I'll have to tell them."

"Oh, for Christ's sake. That's it? That's your reason for not going? What a fucking lame excuse."

"And what if you go, and I go, and they keep you on. Then what? Do we stay there forever? For the rest of our lives? That's it?"

"Jesus Christ. You'd think I was asking you to climb on my funeral pyre. No, that's not it. We decide together. One vote each. Or you can come back if you aren't happy. To your wonderful life in London. And keep writing about bloody Fabergé eggs till they carry you out of that room in a box." So we were at it again, though without the demonic energy, more like a middle-aged couple who'd been airing the same grudges and grievances for years. Finally, I stood up, I put my coat back on, and this time he didn't try to stop me.

"I'll phone you in the morning," I said.

"Fine. Super. Happy dreams."

Just then the phone rang. "Hey, Gareth," Jack said, turning his back on me. I paused in the doorway as he started scribbling on an old envelope—flight numbers, phone numbers? "Three six two one—got it. Great, I'll give them a ring." It was plain from his voice that he knew I hadn't left; he was giving a demonstration, for my benefit, of that buoyant optimism he had enjoined on me. "Wilding...okay...terrific." I couldn't listen anymore; I went and let myself out, thinking, as I headed downstairs, that this might be the last time I would walk down those ratty steps, the last time I would yank at that eternally stuck front door to open it. Already nostalgia was setting in. Pretty soon a certain kind of Northern accent would make me go all wistful; those rants of his I had claimed to hate would take on a sheen of adorableness. I had to resist the urge to go back and throw my arms around him in surrender. Instead I kept on walking, and gradually the cramped little houses I passed en route to the Tube, the dingy curtains fluttering in peeling windows, no longer seemed charged with tragic emotion. When I got to the station, the meat turning on skewers in the kebab shop window, the pale splotchy boy with studs in his nose, the smeared red tiles in the entrance were only themselves, no more vivid or sinister than usual. I was a free woman again.

Sixteen

Isabel looked more than ever like a Florentine Madonna the next time I saw her, thinking herself unobserved at a long table in the North Reading Room, with a stack of unopened books beside her. She was staring into space, her chin resting on her hand, her cheeks flushed, while a bald little man opposite was casting furtive glances her way, more wistful than lecherous, as though trying to remember what happiness felt like.

In a dim corner of my brain I registered that she was different, but my need to unburden myself was too pressing for anything else to get through. Two days earlier Jack had returned from America, contract in hand, bringing me a catalogue from the Walker Art Center of photographs of grain elevators, as though that might persuade me. We had been up half the night, not hurling insults and jumping up and down but thrashing things out in a spirit of sorrowful inquiry: why couldn't I at least give it a try? What was the hang-up, the lingering childhood trauma, the still extant fantasy, that fueled my reluctance? What was I so afraid of losing?

And finally, did I or didn't I love him, how did I *feel*, in the deep heart's core? I was a woman, an American; apparently those things combined should have ensured a certain intimacy with my own feelings. I had a fleeting memory of Julian saying something similar, in his jeering way. Even to remember Julian made me want to hurl myself at Jack and promise always to be true.

At three a.m. he delivered an ultimatum—a deadline, he called it, pointing out that I'd always said how much I needed them. "A fortnight. Two weeks from today." I felt his weight lifting off the mattress, I heard his footsteps retreating and then returning. "If you stay you may as well take over the flat," he said gruffly. "I'll have to pay rent through June anyway, or the department will."

I rolled over. "Thank you . . . really. Thank you. I'm sorry I'm such a ditherer."

"You are. You're a right ditherer."

When he was sweet like that, it was harder than ever to hold out. I imagined him surrounded by worshipful students—all blond, since I still thought of everyone in Minnesota as blond—charmed by his English accent and his battered satchel and his rants about old Etonians. If I phoned him in a month and announced that I was coming, he might tell me not to bother. Or he might say, "Let's talk about that some other time, I'm just dashing out the door," and I would know from the embarrassment in his voice, his uncharacteristic evasiveness, that it was too late.

That was the scenario his friend Hester outlined
for me with great force and vividness. It was at the dinner parties of Hester and her journalist husband that
I had first told my stories of the earl and the model
trains. Hester had also given me an account of Isabel at Cambridge totally different from Isabel's own.
Isabel had conjured up an absurd figure—in her first
year, she said, she'd been so consumed with love for
a theology student she used to walk over to his college
at night and stare up at his lighted windows, hoping to
catch a glimpse of him. "Really, I think, he was simply
dreary, a kind of Casaubon character, but I thought he
was noble and pure. He had a very high forehead, that
was probably it. And elastoplasts all over his hands,
because he worked in a shelter for rescue dogs, and
they quite often bit him."

But according to Hester, who had been on the
same corridor at Girton, she had been famous as the
most beautiful girl in their year. (I felt a ridiculous
burst of pride when she said this.) "A lesbian poet
who later got sent down for selling drugs wrote a
whole series of Dada sonnets about her, called 'The
Zaza of the Golden Zygomatics.' And of course we
all knew who her mother was. But she was mostly very
quiet, a bit recessive, really, she wasn't exactly a party
girl. Not like me . . . I was awfully wild in those days,
believe it or not. Sowing my oats before the gong
went." Hester had MS; for the past five years she'd
been in a wheelchair, while continuing to practice
Gestalt therapy and meddle in her friends' lives. She

had phoned me several times while Jack was away, to urge me to go to Minneapolis. She had so many friends, she said, so many clients, who regretted the chances they'd thrown away when they still thought they had time. Did I want to grow old alone, did I know how hard it was for women as they aged? I was making a terrible mistake, making him beg me, I mustn't humiliate him like that.

"So you're saying this is it for me, right? The last hurrah."

"I just worry that you're not very *realistic*, poppet. And of course that's part of what we all love about you, but isn't it time to start thinking about your future? It's fine to live from day to day when you're in your twenties, but...you aren't, are you? You're getting close to your sell-by date."

Over watery coffee in the museum cafeteria, I poured out my woes to Isabel. It was almost a repeat of that first time, only now there was something impersonal and remote about her sympathy, all her responses were one beat too late. Even when she said she'd miss me dreadfully if I went, but that was just selfishness, of course I must do whatever was best for me, it sounded like mere good manners, the correct sentiment to express under the circumstances: there was no sign of distress at the prospect of my leaving. I got the feeling I was boring her, but I pushed on, hungry for the balm of connection.

"Hester says I'd be crazy not to go. She's convinced he'll find someone else two weeks after he hits town."

"Oh, Hester," Isabel said absently.

"It's odd, isn't it, that she's so convinced of the fickleness of men. Nobody ever had a more devoted husband than Paul."

"But think of the price of that devotion. Having to be eternally grateful. And everyone saying what a saint he is." Her attention wandered to the people at the next table, a frazzled-looking middle-aged woman in a brown felt hat and a girl with stubby purple fingernails. The woman was making what looked like a desperate effort at persuasion, while the girl stared sulkily at the tablecloth and said nothing.

"She must be her daughter," Isabel said. "It's that look daughters get when their mothers are trying to warn them not to hitchhike to Marrakesh or drop out of university and join a rock band." I sat there in silence for a minute, watching her watch them with an air of smothered excitement that surely had nothing to do with those people. At any moment, it seemed, she might start humming a little tune under her breath. Then I remembered.

"How was your trip to Oxford?" And suddenly she was wholly present.

"It was extraordinary," she said, flushing; then, primly, "I mean, the papers. So fascinating to see how the Russians managed to incorporate the Indian mathematicians' ideas into their work. The concept of divine numbers. I'd never thought before how deterministic calculus is. I mean, all that emphasis on continuous functions. It really is a denial of spirituality."

"Right. Continuous functions. Very unspiritual. How was Alexei?"

"Oh," she said, biting her lip, and then started over, her voice dropping a little. "I think he's having a quite bad time of it. He's had to mortgage his house to finance his work, now that they've cut his funding. But he's still not sure he can keep going much longer. And then there's a kind of cabal among the mathematicians, they spread the most vile rumors about him. It's ghastly, what those people are capable of." I recognized the proprietary note of sorrow—a way of talking about loving someone without coming out and saying so. It was what women did, they luxuriated in pity; I knew about that. But she wasn't supposed to be one of those women. And I couldn't help thinking that Alexei had been looking after himself perfectly fine for years, even done rather well, all things considered.

I shifted in my chair. "So when are you going to see him again?"

She didn't know, she said, maybe some time the following week, when he was due to come to London to talk to someone at UC. "Perhaps we should all get together," she added politely.

"That's all right. I really should be working on the article anyway. Tell him I'll send it to him when I'm done."

"Oh, yes, do. I know how much he's looking forward to reading it."

She was starting to exasperate me. I even had the unworthy feeling that I had a right to know what the hell was going on: I had introduced them, after all. But it was more than that; it was her air of exaltation, of keeping a precious secret, as though the whole thing had some holy significance that I couldn't be expected to understand. As though I might taint its purity with my deterministic calculus.

"Come to the pub," I said. "It would be a good deed on your part—I'm sick of my own thoughts, I need some distraction." Once we were sitting with drinks in front of us I did manage to get some details out of her, exploiting the evident pleasure it gave her just to say his name out loud.

It sounded as though he hadn't been a bit lover-like, I could have predicted that. But I'll bet he kept his eyes fixed on hers the whole time he was holding forth, as though it was the most urgent matter in the world that she should believe in his Russians too. So it was a kind of wooing after all.

Apart from that, it seemed as though he mostly just scolded her—for not caring what kind of wine she drank (they went to some restaurant on the river; I was dying to ask who had paid), for not being concerned enough about what a mess the world was in (and hence, I suppose, how much it needed the Russians' spiritual wisdom). He even scolded her about Lucy, who had decided, some time back, that she would not go to university, but instead would join a program that trained people to help sink wells in rural areas of Africa where children died from drinking dirty water. I had already heard about that from Isabel: "She said she wasn't talking about some gap-year project, she means to take on that sort of work for life. Not exactly what I wanted for her, I would have loved her to go to Cambridge and be hailed as a genius, but I have to admire her for it." I had dutifully expressed admiration too, though privately I'd wondered how long she'd last.

Alexei, though, was incensed at the idea. This was nonsense, he said. Lucy had a moral obligation to use her brains: the first duty was always to the things of the mind, it was this that distinguished humans from the animals. "I detest all this modern sentimentality, this denial of the intellect in favor of the heart. It is very American." (Isabel quoted this to me verbatim, in a passable imitation of his accent, screwing up her face in disgust just the way he did. I remembered how she used to imitate the Sidworth guests for Maddy. But when she "did" Alexei her face was alight.) Animals had hearts, he said, adding that he had the highest respect for animals, they had many skills that humans lacked. "But the most deeply human, the most deeply moral thing we can do is to think truly." And when she said she wasn't so sure of that, he told her she was very stupid, and roared with laughter. She too must have been corrupted by the Americans, he said, he saw now that she was a secret sentimentalist. Which of course was what her mother always accused her of.

By this time she was enjoying the memory too much to need any further prodding.

He became very stern, she said, he insisted that the glorification of feelings was not only wrong, it was dangerous: "'Feelings are not so pretty, they are primitive things, one must be very careful of them.

Look at the fascists. They knew how to appeal to feeling, they made the people believe that way, they took away the responsibility to think.'

"He said the Americans have adopted a similar tactic for their own purposes, their corporations are numbing people's brains with constant entertainment, lulling them into a state of mindless pleasure, so that they can take over the world."

"Yes, he gave me his rap about America too. Apparently the University of Texas made him an offer for the papers, but he decided he couldn't possibly let them go to America, he couldn't be sure they wouldn't put some of the equations to evil use. It's a little weird, actually, when you think of all that stuff the Communists did to him, that he sees America as the root of all evil."

"Oh, but I even said that to him. I tried to tease him about it a little, though I don't think he cares for being teased. He thinks it's a bad habit the English have, we pride ourselves on making a joke of everything, he says, we're all terribly frivolous. Oh dear. Anyway, he said he wasn't a Communist, he was a Marxist, which is quite different. And I suppose it is really. He told me some dreadful things about the American corporations and the Nazis."

He had told me some of that too: how "Mr. Rockefeller's Standard Oil" was shipping fuel to the Germans through Switzerland, long after America entered the war. He had a plethora of such facts at his disposal, proof positive of the marriage of corporate

and political power around the globe, how it super-
seded all national considerations. And interspersed
with these harangues were handy quotes from Dosto-
yevsky about the need to annihilate the ego.

I had found myself so irritated by his multiple
certainties that I'd wound up arguing with him out
of sheer cussedness, even when he had me half convinced. But maybe he reminded her of Stavros, who
was full of judgment too, who had told her that Cavafy
was a fascist. And of course, like Stavros, he was so un-
English; he took everything seriously, not just Ivanov's
final notebook entry, on the transcendent reality of
perfect mathematical entities, which I'm sure he dis-
coursed on over dinner, but even the choice of wine,
and following that what food they would eat.

Anyway, despite the moral imperative of thinking,
I suspect desire was interfering with her judgment,
as I had seen happening during our lunch. Probably
he'd sat there frowning at the wine list as though it was
a particularly knotty theorem, and maybe, as she sat
watching him, she wasn't worrying about determinism
or the depredations of Standard Oil.

She did tell me, blushing, that because he felt she
wasn't eating enough—"I think you are one of these
modern women, always on a diet"—he began feeding
her from his own plate. But then she quickly changed
the subject, launching into the tale of his childhood,
which actually I had heard already, from him, though
I didn't say so: from the tremor in her voice, I got the
sense she thought of it as a precious confidence, not

something he made a point of telling any woman he met, which was what I suspected. It was, after all, his ultimate credential, the ace in the pack.

And in fact it would take a very hard heart not to be moved by that story, one of famine and starvation, of people dying by the thousands. It had happened not during the war, but after it, he'd told me. The roadsides in Rostov were picked clean of grass, the trees were stripped of their leaves, there were no birds anywhere: everything had been eaten; the bodies of the dead were shoveled into carts and taken away to be burned. There was talk of neighbors eating neighbors, cutting the bodies open to remove the livers and hearts. He had made it his job to forage for food for himself and his mother, which meant walking miles out of the city, to where the collective farms were. (Some of that land had belonged to his mother's father, who had been denounced as a class enemy, and shot with other kulaks, during the collectivization in the thirties.) If he was lucky, he could just manage to wriggle beneath the barbed wire erected to protect the crops—he was already six or seven at the time, but very small for his age ("all the children born during the war were small"). He was very proud to be the one feeding them, though his mother was terrified: adults caught stealing even a few ears of wheat could be sent to prison for a year; for a few kilograms of grain, or three potatoes, they might get eight years in the gulag. But to him it was a wonderful game, he'd told her, he felt like a hero in an old ballad.

And was Isabel remembering the greenhouses at Sidworth, with the asparagus and tomatoes, the grapes growing up one wall, the apricot trees in their handsome pots? Or the lambs that grazed in the pastures along the drive every spring, and the joints of beef from the farmer's Angus cows that hung in the cold room in the cellar? How Nanny used to tell her, when she wouldn't eat her porridge, that there were starving children all over the world who would be grateful to have such lovely porridge to eat? Now she was sitting across from one of those mythic children, longing— not that she told me this—to be in bed with him. He had not touched her once, remember, not even brushed her hand.

I imagine her returning to her house that night, going to the mirror in the front hall to see if her lipstick had all smudged away, and whether her hair was a mess. Maybe she took out the pins that held it and shook it until it fell down past her shoulders. For more than a year it would have been Lucy's absence she felt when she walked in; now maybe there was something more, a different sense of aloneness. And if she went into the sitting room and picked up the photo of Stavros from the side table then, she may have seen, more clearly than ever before, how young he looked. They had both been so young. If he had lived he would not be that person anymore, just as she was no longer the person he'd known in Athens.

Or maybe she just wandered through the rooms, imagining how they would look to Alexei—deciding to have the kitchen repainted, or the cracked ceiling in the sitting room repaired, thinking about buying pale pink sheets, because her flesh would look so rosy against them. Planning which books to have on the coffee table, that he would approve of. Wondering when he'd phone, where they would meet, what she would wear. Thinking he might phone the next day, even. All the old, heart-twisting banalities, which no amount of irony defends against. Anyway, for the next few months irony would be suspended, just when it was most needed. And by the time it returned, by the time I heard the full story from her in Jack's flat, it was all over.

Seventeen

S he was not in the habit of confiding in her mother; in fact the opposite was true. You could say that keeping things from Helena was part of her survival strategy. But despite Helena's age and infirmity, she still had a little network in Oxford, elderly dons who phoned when there was a particularly juicy bit of gossip: a philosopher who'd been writing indecent letters to a colleague's wife, a regius professor caught plagiarizing whole paragraphs from an obscure Italian scholar. Now it seemed one of her informants had spotted Isabel in a restaurant on the river with a man he described as a very unsavory Russian. "Not only that, but he was shoveling food into your mouth, while you were giggling like a schoolgirl."

There was a whole litany of charges against Alexei that Helena went on to repeat: he had no degree in maths or anything else, he had wheedled his way into the university by lying about his qualifications, he had squandered vast sums on elaborate computer systems he had no idea how to use. But those were trivial compared to the final allegation: he had somehow charmed a distinguished old woman in Cambridge,

widow of one of Darwin's descendants, into alter-
ing her will and leaving a large part of her fortune to
his project; after her death, he had been sued by her
children for undue influence and manipulation, and
an out-of-court settlement had been reached. "Who
knows?" Helena said. "Perhaps he murdered her, it
happens far more often than people realize. One only
hears about the incompetent killers, who get caught,
the clever ones get away with it. Some drops of azalea
nectar in her sherry might have done it. Or rhodo-
dendron leaves stirred into her tea. Those Russian
peasants know all about the uses of plants."

That was preposterous, Isabel told her, out of the
question, and anyway, Alexei had already explained
about the ugly rumors that were swirling around
him (though in fact he hadn't mentioned widows or
lawsuits). "He had as great a passion for his work as
she did for hers, I said, if she met him she would
see that, it wasn't something he could fake. And I
reminded her what the academic world was like; after
all, there'd been a lot of viciousness and backbiting
about her too, she ought to have some sympathy for
him, she shouldn't automatically believe every ugly
rumor that was floating around. Especially not if it
came from Gerald, who's a notorious gossip. But she
totally dismissed that, she said it was all to do with my
age, I was just at that dangerous time in a woman's
life when she makes a fool of herself over a man. She
was worried about me, she said, I needed to be pro-
tected from myself."

Meanwhile I was wondering, half guiltily, if there could possibly be any truth to the story of the widow. Perhaps it was my journalistic duty to make inquiries, though I wasn't sure how I'd go about it: would there be court records if a settlement had been reached? I scribbled a note to myself on the pad by the telephone. But I never followed up.

Of course Alexei had told me, as he'd told Isabel, about the "cabal" of mathematicians who were trying to discredit him. When I'd questioned what could possibly be motivating them—thinking I could add paranoia to the list of his peculiarities—he'd said they were afraid that the papers of the Name Worshippers, once published, would show up their own trivial work for the poor thing it was. As for the transcription systems: three separate software programs had needed to be modified and combined before they could accurately replicate the deeply idiosyncratic notational system the men had used.

"I ask myself, should I step aside now, will all this pettiness then cease, this shadow that blocks out the sun? But no: the timid little academics who succeed me will censor the manuscripts, or bury the really radical passages in appendices, or they will seek to discredit their most important message by saying these men were religious fanatics, not mentally sound. In the very act of publishing their views they will dismiss them, so that nobody need take notice of their argument about the rationalists' arrogance, how it destroys the relations of man and nature. They will present their work as a mere footnote to the true mathematics, the sort they do themselves. And then all the other sheep will see it that way, it will be shunted aside." It was not, he'd told me, that nobody else could do his work, that was very far from the case, almost anybody could do it. No, it was that nobody else *would*. "I cannot abandon these thinkers whom I respect above all others, whose writings rescued me from despair." All these remarks I was scrupulously quoting in my article, neither advocating for his point of view nor debunking it, though I had to acknowledge that, whatever the truth of his claims for the Name Worshippers, he at least seemed to believe them.

Helena, however, wasn't about to give him the benefit of the doubt. "Whether or not he was in the habit of slipping poison into people's drinks, she said, he was obviously an extremely dodgy character. And then she went on to extrapolate from my previous history. How I had a positive passion for displaced persons. Meaning Stavros, of course, who wasn't displaced at all, as I pointed out; he was exactly where he was meant to be. 'But not an accepted member of society,' she said. Never mind that it was a fascist dictatorship; the accepted members of society were the liars and torturers. But she didn't want to hear that. I was unhealthily attracted to outcasts, she said, it was downright morbid. Actually, I suspect she still secretly feels that anyone who's not English is an outcast. Which might even include you.

"I didn't understand what those people were like, she said, I was far too trusting. 'He's after something from you, that much is perfectly obvious.' Which was her constant refrain in my childhood. If she didn't like the girls I brought back to the house, she'd say they were only pretending to be my friends, they just wanted to boast that they'd been to Sidworth, or their mothers had sent them to nose around, they wanted to find out who was staying with us, who was sleeping in which bedroom. She'd claim she was trying to protect me then too, she was sorry for me, she said, I couldn't see when I was being taken advantage of.

"But at some point I realized she never talked that way about the girls who flattered her, the ones who told her how much they'd enjoyed her talk on Radio Four, or admired the portrait of her grandfather. Probably they'd been primed, their parents had instructed them what to say, but that never occurred to her. In fact the girl she disliked most was the last person to care about the sleeping arrangements at Sidworth. She was my best friend at school, she barely noticed her surroundings, she really did live in her head, which was stuffed full of literature, she could recite reams of poetry at age fifteen. I think Mother just made her nervous, she'd mumble Hello and then we'd go upstairs to my room and have long earnest discussions about whether if you changed one phrase in a poem you had two separate poems, because you'd altered the organic unity of the whole. That sort of thing. Mother insisted she was sly and underhanded, and told me she had proof that Gwen was supplying Sasha with drugs, which I knew was a lie. But she refused to have her in the house anymore.

"That was the spring when the situation with Sasha had become desperate. My little talk with her about her genes had only made things worse, she seemed more determined than ever to blow holes in her DNA with any drug the local yobs could supply. When Mother remonstrated with her Sasha just stood there, her face would go all stony, she'd narrow her eyes and fix them on a point just past Mother's shoulder. And then if Mother lectured her on her heritage, those excellent nucleotides she'd been so concerned to provide for her, Sasha would yelp with laughter. Or she'd start humming louder and louder, to drown Mother out. It occurs to me now that of all the people in Mother's life till then, Sasha was the only one who defeated her, the single person she couldn't bring under her control. No wonder she had to be sent away."

Eighteen

Maybe she was just infatuated with Alexei at that point, only halfway to love—teetering on the brink. But that was before the miracle occurred, the single thing guaranteed to clinch the deal: he restored Sasha to sanity.

"Oh, come on," I said. "That's ridiculous."

"Of course I don't suppose it will last forever, I'm not that naive, but really, it was extraordinary to see the difference in her when they were talking. It made me realize she's right, I'm always humoring her, or placating her ... trying to fend off her attacks, like a matador with a charging bull. Even when she's *not* on the attack. I never speak to her naturally, the way I would to you. It's a pattern that got fixed between us years ago, and I've never managed to break it. But I'm going to try."

"You sound positively evangelical ... Isn't that another thing Sasha always says, that you should have been a missionary? Never mind. How did this miracle come about? I'm all ears."

It seemed that Alexei had been sleeping beside her that morning—she lowered her eyes as she told me this—when Sasha rang at 5:30 or some ungodly hour.

"She wanted me to go see her, she said Daphne was going to her uncle's funeral that day, down in Surrey, and she'd been having bad dreams, she didn't want to stay there alone. But she wouldn't tell me what the dreams were about. She just rambled on, about rhubarb crumble, and Daphne's uncle, how he'd go straight to Heaven because he used to rescue people's cats when they'd climbed up a tree. She was thinking of getting a cat, she said, that would torture her, and she'd torture it back. And then she said she was tired of living in her body, she didn't want it anymore, she was going to sell it and go to America on the proceeds, how much did I think she'd get for it? The last time she talked about getting rid of her body she wound up in hospital a week later. So I said all right, I'd come see her later that morning."

She'd had no intention of taking Alexei, she said, it didn't even occur to her, but he was awake when she got back to bed, so she had to explain. "He wanted to know all about her, the whole story. And then he said he'd come with me, which I told him wasn't a good idea at all, not when she was so distraught, but he said . . ."—she took a breath, her voice went soft—"he said that was why he'd proposed it, because she was distraught. 'Sometimes a stranger can make a diversion,' he said. He knew that from experience, he told me, in Russia after the war there were many women whose minds were shattered because of the terrible things that had happened. And his mother used to take him to see them."

But when they got there, Sasha was just as enraged at her having brought a stranger as she'd known she'd be. "I truly thought for a minute she was going to claw his eyes out; she told him to get out, she shouted at him that she didn't want him in her flat, and when he just stood there calmly, she looked as though she was about to hurl herself at him. But after a few minutes she calmed down, I think it was because he wasn't frightened of her, it made me realize how much she counts on scaring people. He smiled at her so kindly, until finally she just shrugged and went into the sitting room, and sat down on the floor. And then he sat down facing her."

It sounded a little creepy to me, almost like some kind of est-type California therapy. Alexei as guru: was that one of his sidelines? Did he start chanting, did he hypnotize her? But apparently it was just the opposite, he treated Sasha's problem as purely intellectual, not psychological at all. He was going to argue her out of her Cartesian delusion, the wicked fallacy in Enlightenment thought that at its most extreme could lead someone to believe she could abandon her body like a parcel at a left luggage office. He would show her the path out of the thicket in which she was caught, that quicksand, he called it, in which she could only sink deeper and deeper; she must be made to see that there was no split, there were no such categories as subject and object, et cetera, et cetera. Once she understood that, her torment would be no more.

"Let me guess...and then he told her about his Russians."

"Yes."

"And their heroic struggles, and their spiritual revelations."

"Don't be horrid. You mustn't sneer at him, he believes in them so passionately. And he might even have a point. Actually I thought Sasha would sneer, nothing brings out her mockery more than someone being solemn. But she was fascinated. She was a maths prodigy, remember, she understood the specifics of it much better than I had. She made him write out equations for her, maybe it was proofs, and then she'd snatch the paper from him and nod and frown exactly the way he did. Honestly, she was completely sane at that point. Whether it was the maths or him I don't know, but it made me ashamed of how I tiptoe around her madness, I'm not real with her the way he was. She said such a touching thing to him at one point: 'I hope Issy never goes mad,' she said, 'I don't think she could handle it. But you'd do all right with it. You might even find it quite interesting.'

"Of course, once he realized what a clever student he'd got hold of, he couldn't resist reeling off whole lists of things she ought to read. Gottlob Frege and all those people. She was done with the logicians, she told him, if anything could make her go mad again it was reading them, but he kept insisting, until finally she said, 'What a bossy boots you are.' Which got them onto a whole other subject, because he'd never heard that expression. The English vernacular was very puzzling to him, he told her, so many things about the English puzzled him, perhaps she could enlighten him on these matters. 'You'd better ask Issy,' she said, 'I'm a certified lunatic, remember?' But it was precisely because she was a lunatic—he didn't say no, no, she wasn't a lunatic, the way I would have, he used the word perfectly cheerfully—that she could be most helpful to him, he said; she would have observed the customs of her own people the way an alien might, she would not merely accept the conventional wisdom."

"So did she proceed to enlighten him? I'd love to know what she said."

Here are some of the topics it seems they covered: nicknames—should he call Isabel Issy, should he call a student who was helping him with the manuscripts, whose name was Charles Frinton, Fritters, the name someone had used once in asking for him on the phone? Would that be a friendly thing to do, would it make for a more informal relation between them? (No, Sasha said, it was probably the name he'd been given in school, and only his very old friends still called him that.) Why were the English so keen on these nicknames, he wanted to know, was it because they could not show their affection in any other way? Was it true that they did not hug their children, that they did not cry at funerals? Why did they seem so often embarrassed? He sometimes felt he embarrassed them with his very being. If he spoke too seriously, he embarrassed them; if he expressed too much enthusiasm, he embarrassed them. Even if he paid them a compliment, they looked embarrassed. And when he jostled them in the street, why did they say "Sorry"? Shouldn't he be the one who was sorry?

"Which made Sasha laugh like anything. He wasn't getting out enough, she said; all those old clichés might be true of Oxford people, but there was a whole other England out there, he ought to travel around and see it. 'Not half so self-conscious. That's one of the advantages of the bin, you really do meet all sorts in there,' she told him. Some English people did hug their children and cry at funerals. As for nicknames, it probably had something to do with a nostalgia for childhood. It was a great national obsession, she said, everybody yearning for lost innocence, purity, some species of prelapsarian grace. *Paradise Lost. The Land of Lost Content.*

"He was terribly pleased with that idea. 'You see?' he told her. 'I knew you would have something intelligent to say on the subject.' Then, triumphantly, 'What about Peter Pan?' And Sasha said, of course, how could she have forgotten Peter Pan. They were having a lovely time together, I could almost have been jealous. Because I don't think either of them would have minded awfully if I hadn't been there."

Later, because the sun was shining, he announced that they must go out and enjoy it like proper English people. (He had already refused Sasha's offer of coffee, because he disapproved of her coffee maker. Were all Russians as rude as he was? she wanted to know.)

And so they went to Kensington Gardens, home to Peter Pan in bronze, surrounded by adorable bunny rabbits and squirrels and fairies (the statue was a disgrace, Alexei said, while admiring the railings around the Italian Gardens, stooping down to see how they'd been constructed. "Don't tell me you're a blacksmith too," Sasha said). They watched the little boys sail their boats on the Round Pond, and the swans and ducks snap greedily at the yellow peas sprinkled on the water by an old woman in a battered straw hat. A golden retriever, tail wagging madly, came and laid a stick at Sasha's feet. All this Isabel described to me in a voice bright with remembered happiness: the three of them, replete with sun and pleasure, almost a family, lingering by the carousel, listening to the children's excited shouts. And planning to visit the Russian mosaics and costumes at the V&A sometime, because he'd never been. "It was quite magical really. I can't remember the last time I felt so extraordinarily light."

I, on the other hand, felt sour and grouchy as I listened. The whole thing was too beautiful to be real, a fairy tale among the flowerbeds, with Alexei as the avatar of grace. Each time she saw him, it seemed, he became nobler in her eyes. The crusader for spiritual awakening, the brave hungry child in a war-torn country, the victim of malice and persecution all his adult life. Now this dubious-sounding miracle with Sasha.

Descartes or no, she was brimming over like a schoolgirl with a crush. I felt embarrassed for her, unable to respond to this new effervescence. Even the "extraordinary" lightness was the tiredest of clichés—walking on air, the stuff of a hundred bad songs. I missed the old Isabel—her wryness, the slight melancholy she'd worn so lightly it was a form of serenity. (And what if all along it hadn't been serenity, just sadness, gracefully contained? What if under the melancholy lay real hopelessness? Wasn't she as entitled as the next person to make a fool of herself? But I didn't see it like that at the time.)

She did tell me there'd been an awkward moment at the end. Sasha insisted she wanted to drive Isabel's car back to her flat, and Isabel refused—Sasha always drove too fast, she said. Sasha turned on her then, calling her a priss, trotting out the missionary line. She appealed to Alexei: couldn't he just imagine Issy as one of those Victorians in Africa, didn't he think the natives would have got fed up with her, and boiled her into a tasty stew? Wouldn't he like to see how she drove? She was much better than Isabel, she knew what a car was for. But he just shook his head and refused to be drawn in. So Sasha sat down abruptly on the grass and refused to budge. Finally, to stop the afternoon from going pear-shaped, Isabel promised that on their next outing she could drive, as long as she gave her word to keep within the speed limit. Sasha made her swear she meant it, and then she got up and they walked together to the car. I would have occasion to remember that exchange later on.

Nineteen

All through my pregnancy my dreams were rich and vivid, everything brilliantly colored, more lifelike than life. The bathtub was full of worms, a huge wave was sweeping the house out to sea. Jack and I were rolling Easter eggs down a hill, or struggling across rough terrain with a suitcase full of frying pans. I gave birth to a leg of lamb, to Rumpelstiltskin, to a dog. There was nothing dreamlike about those apparitions; when I dragged myself out of the heavy sleep I slept then, to stumble into the bathroom and pee, the images were still there between me and the light.

My father appeared, thin and nervy as ever, the same age he'd been when he left, but dressed like a circus clown, or sometimes a priest, clutching a prayer book, asking me if I'd care to dance. As we waltzed around the church hall, he explained his departure to me, why he'd had to go, and all of it made perfect sense, a great peace descended, though the next morning I couldn't remember anything he'd said. Eliot walked down Twenty-Third Street at my side, explaining the obstruction rule in baseball, or steering me around a puddle. Of all the people I dreamt of

then, Eliot was the least transformed, as solidly himself as ever, his substance intact even in death. When
Isabel appeared, though, she was elusive, wraithlike,
a shade from one of her Greek myths, flitting down
hallways in a vast drafty house, or through the woods
behind the house in Gurneyville, while I staggered
after her in a hopeless game of hide-and-seek, and
when I woke up I was crying.

But hadn't she been a little like that when she
was alive, hadn't the dream conveyed a truth just as
my dreams of Eliot did? The hunt I dreamed about:
there'd definitely been times when I'd felt she was elud-
ing me, I couldn't pin her down. I couldn't even be
sure which Isabel I was crying for, the graceful exalted
one or the woman sobbing on Jack's smelly couch the
last time I saw her. She had pretty much told me herself that night that she wasn't what I'd imagined.

"Come on," Jack said. "There's no great mystery
about it. She was your Sebastian Flyte, your adolescent fantasy come to life." But he said it without
rancor. His grievances, even against the English, had
largely evaporated, leaving him much less harsh in his
judgments.

He'd never felt so free, he told me; he'd never realized how cramped and fettered he'd felt in his London life until he left it behind. "All that petty sniping
and backbiting that went on at Birkbeck, I was so used
to it I just assumed it was normal. There's nothing like
that at the U." (He loved to call it the U, just as he
loved to say elevator, and trunk and hood instead of

boot and bonnet: he had easily learned to drive on the other side of the road.)

He'd even forgiven the lie I told him when I phoned to say I was joining him—I'd been so afraid he wouldn't take me back that I said I was pregnant. Two months later I was.

He would bundle me solicitously into his old shitbox—"shitbox" was another word he loved—and head up 95 to the open spaces of the St. Croix Valley. We'd park on a certain hill on County Road F and look down on a vast expanse of bright blue water, dazzling in the sunlight, a view he never tired of. Even the green-and-white signs on the thruway elicited hymns of praise; they were so beautifully placed, so large and bright, suspended across the highway so that nobody could miss them; "In England they'd be the size of a matchbox, and stuck off to one side, half covered by some tree. Here, it's as though they actually *want* you to get where you're going, they care."

"Oh honestly, that's absurd." But only occasionally did I point out that his romance with America was no more realistic than mine with England, about which he'd always been so scathing. Did he truly believe that the friendliness of Bill in the minimart was a sincere expression of goodwill? And how could he stand to hang out with Mrs. Swanson, our busybody of a landlady, who always referred to him as the professor, who kept assuring me, though I hadn't expressed concern, that the baby could cry as much as it liked, she was half-deaf anyway. On my more recessive days, I'd lurk behind the blind in the bathroom and watch for Mrs. Swanson to leave the house before going downstairs to collect the mail, so she couldn't pop out of her door and invite me in for coffee. Jack, on the other hand, would cheerfully spend half of Saturday morning in her kitchen, munching Oreos while she reminisced to him about the drunken Indian who'd worked for her father back in North Dakota when she was a kid, or the time her late husband had hit the jackpot on a three-wheel slot machine in Vegas.

I knew it couldn't last, all that sweetness and light, the ardor for his adopted country that even the spectacle of Dan Quayle and Jimmy Swaggart on the evening news failed to dampen. I knew that sooner or later his Old World skepticism would return, his exuberance was bound to die down. But meanwhile it was strangely restful, living with his good cheer; it required so little effort from me—no need to coax him out of a funk, expostulate, protest that things weren't really that terrible. He was the hunter-gatherer, foraging in the wide world, keeping us safe, while I stayed at home with his baby growing in my belly, reading old books and having sudden mad fits of house cleaning. There was something primeval—shamefully, luxuriantly so—about it, a surrender to will-lessness I knew I might never achieve again.

By mid-October, the leaves were long gone; the real blizzards had not yet arrived, but there was already a dusting of snow on the ground. I was dreading the winter, which I'd always hated as a child; I'd started to dream of struggling across vast sinister expanses of ice with a hundred-pound weight on my back. Jack's colleagues at the U kept warning him that he didn't know what he was in for. But however many stories they told of cars stuck in ten-foot drifts, roofs torn off, whole families found frozen in isolated farmhouses, he was undaunted. "Everyone should experience a real, proper winter like that at least once."

From the beginning, I had been introduced as his fiancée, in case anyone objected to our cohabiting. Once I was pregnant, the issue of health insurance became pressing. Magnificent coverage was offered to faculty spouses, we discovered, poring over the brochures describing the program with the awe we might have devoted to an auction catalogue of Old Masters. So one Wednesday morning—he didn't teach on Wednesdays, or have office hours—we drove to City Hall in the shitbox and after a brief argument about where to park exchanged our vows, assuring each other that it was a strictly practical step, taken for insurance reasons alone; it would not alter anything. But with or without the benefit of clergy, with or without rings and garlands, even with only a paid witness to offer congratulations, there is something biblical about marriage, like wading into a river after splashing in shallow streams. I'd felt it with Eliot, despite everything; I felt it even more now.

And still there were things I never talked about, like my last weeks in London, when I was living alone in his flat in Tufnell Park. I never told him about the night Isabel came, or the story of Alexei, or the scene in the hospital when I went to visit Sasha. That might have disturbed the peace—or it might have felt like too great a betrayal. Because what if it awakened all the old resentments again, what if he thundered on at me about the decadence of the upper classes? There was no defense I could have made. But even if he was right, everything he said was true, it could never be the whole truth—not mine, anyway.

Twenty

I was the one who insisted she come, though I wasn't sure I meant it; I doubted my sincerity till the minute I opened the door and saw her face.

She didn't refer to what she'd told me on the phone; she was painfully polite, her movements precise in the way drunks' are when they're trying to walk straight. "It was so kind of you to invite me," she said, in a high plummy voice, like an actor's in a period drama, and then, looking around the living room, which I'd been tidying frantically ever since we got off the phone, "what a charming desk," that being the one object it was remotely possible to praise: an old rolltop Jack had found in a junkshop and stripped of several layers of green paint.

"Yes, it is nice, isn't it," I said idiotically, and then, to fill the silence, I told her about Jack and the paint.

"Oh, it must have looked horrid in green," she said, still in that voice (could it be her real one? the way of talking she'd deliberately rid herself of years before?).

"Would you like a cup of tea? I'm afraid I don't have anything else."

"That would be lovely." I told her to sit, waving an arm at the grubby sofa, covered in an Indian bedspread, from which I had removed a mound of books and papers while I was waiting for her. When I came back, bearing the mug, she was sitting bolt upright, like a proper lady. But her mouth was twisted into an unnatural shape, her hair looked as though it hadn't been combed in days. And I noticed a long smear of white on her gray jacket.

"Aren't you having any?"

"I had some a while ago."

"Oh, I'm so sorry. I didn't mean to put you to any bother. And I must be interrupting your work. It was terribly kind of you to invite me."

"You said that already."

"Did I? I'm sorry."

"You said that already too."

"It's just that I'm so tired," she said, shutting her eyes. I remembered, then, saying the same thing that first day in the Reading Room.

"Drink your tea."

"Yes of course." She opened her eyes. "I'm probably hung over, that's it, I drank quite a bit of whiskey last night."

"Do you want to lie down?"

Another shake of the head. "I hung up on her. I'd just put the phone down when I rang you. But I told you that, didn't I? I told her I hated her, I've never said that before . . . That desk really is lovely. Like something out of Dickens. But you don't like

Dickens, do you? Actually, I never cared for him much either."

"What made you say it now?"

"Really, you know, I think I'd better leave."

"No you shouldn't. Tell me."

"I don't want to become hysterical."

"It's okay. It's fine. You're allowed to be hysterical."

"There was always so much of that sort of thing when I was a child. People storming out of rooms. Shrieking insults. But then I was the boring one. Without a temperament. The mousy sensible one."

"Are you nuts? There's nothing mousy about you."

"You may not be the most impartial judge . . . what was the name of that earl in Suffolk? The one with the freezing castle you thought was so romantic?"

"He has nothing to do with this. Believe me. God. You really do but slenderly know yourself."

She leaned back against the couch, shutting her eyes again, but now there were tears trickling down. "Never mind," she said, in a whisper. "It doesn't matter." I went and got a tissue, and when she didn't take it, wiped her face myself, as gently as I could.

After a minute she sat up again, her eyes open. "She bought off Alexei."

"What do you mean?"

"She paid him to keep away from me. A donation, she said. For the Archive."

"So big deal. So he takes the money and goes on seeing you. What can she do about that?"

"She wouldn't have done it if she hadn't been sure of him. She must have dug up something . . . maybe about that woman. The one he was supposed to have murdered, remember? Or she could just have told him, I'll cover your expenses, and let me know when the edition is ready. I'll make sure it's brought to the attention of the right people. He said how sorry he was. But I don't think he was all that sorry."

"The bastard."

"No. It was right for him. It means he can keep faith with his geniuses."

"Purity of heart is to will one thing."

"Something like that."

"Only you can't have purity of heart and take dirty money."

"I don't suppose her money is dirtier than anyone else's," she said, in her old dry way.

"I meant the conditions attached."

"I knew what you meant...I told her I'd never speak to her again as long as I lived."

"And will you?"

"Oh, yes. She knows it, too. In a few weeks I'll be back at Sidworth to make nice with the nurse, bringing that verbena scent from Penhaligon's the new secretary's so fond of. And Mother will be at her most gracious. She always is when she's won. She'll buy me a flowering cherry for my garden. But oh God"—she shut her eyes again—"oh God, I think maybe I loved him."

"I wish I'd never brought you to that lunch."

"Don't say that. I'm glad I met him. Or I will be some day. But Sasha...on the way back in the car that Sunday she was full of plans. You must see the icons at the V&A, she told him, I'll take you there; you'll have to feed the swans with me sometime; we'll go to the Food Hall together, it's better than any museum. Now I have to tell her that she can't ever see him again. One more possibility that's closed to her. As though she hasn't had enough losses. And it'll just go on and on, nothing ever changes for her." She took the tissue I'd been holding and blew her nose. "I know it doesn't seem that important. But she really was different that day, something about him . . . His Russians were going to heal the world's madness, remember?

"I'll make up some lie, I'll say he went back to Russia, or he's off in America, spreading the word about infinity. I'm quite a good liar, you know, I've had to be. Whereas Sasha never learned . . . she must have skipped that lesson, she was probably playing truant the day it was taught." Her voice was slowing down, getting fainter, she was blurring toward sleep. "Sasha went to Sidworth for the weekend . . . She always wants to . . . then it's a disaster . . . a wreck for days."

Just then the phone rang. It was Jack, calling to tell me about an aging Ford Escort for sale by a history professor's son who was joining the Peace Corps; he had not yet broken the habit of needing to report his daily excitements to me. I took the phone into the bedroom to talk, and when I came back Isabel was asleep, her head dropped on her chest, her breath coming in shuddery sighs. Jack's father's navy blanket was sitting on a chair, waiting to be shipped to America; I tucked it around her as best as I could, fearful of waking her. Then I brought the mug of cold tea into the kitchen, rinsed it out, and went off to bed.

That was just after ten. At 2:39 I was awakened by gasping moans, noises I could not place for a moment, so that I scrambled out of bed in confusion, thinking maybe an animal had broken in. Only when the shock of the cold floor cleared my head did I realize what they were. I don't know how long I stood frozen before they began to soften, die down into gulps and shudders, and I went into the other room. In the moonlight coming through the window—I hadn't drawn the curtains—I could see her quite clearly, huddled against the back of the sofa, her fist pressed against her mouth. For a long moment I was silent, waiting for her to acknowledge my presence. Finally she gave a long ragged sigh and turned her head.

"It's all right," I said blindly, because it was all I could think of, that was what you said when someone was crying. "You're going to be all right."

She nodded dully, fumbling on the table for the Kleenex. "Yes of course. Of course I will."

"Can't you just walk away from her? Turn your back on her for good?"

"I thought I had when I was in Greece. But then I came back, and it started again. Maybe Sasha's got it right after all. If I tell her the truth about Alexei, she'll phone Mother and swear at her, she'll send her letters full of insults...the Grand Dominatrix, that's one she's used. Spider lady. Puppet mistress. And we're the puppets...I can't bear to think about Sasha. She should have had such a different life.

"Mother was triumphant when she had her put away. 'You see what happens to those who defy me.' Not that she said it, she didn't have to, the message was clear: I'd better not cross her or I could wind up like Sasha.

"At least Lucy escaped...I hope that's true, I think it is, I think Lucy will be all right. But the three of us...Do you ever think Julian might go home some night and blow his brains out?"

"That's pretty hard for me to imagine."

She nodded tiredly. "I've probably got it wrong then. I seem to have got so many things wrong...It's very peaceful here, isn't it. Though maybe that's just because it's not my house."

"Actually I think it's because it's three in the morning."

She gave a shaky laugh. Then she said, "Thank you. Really. Please let me say it, you've been so kind."

"It's not kindness, it's...think of it as repayment. If that doesn't sound too crass. A thank you in return. I just wish I could think of something wise and beautiful to say, but I can't, there's no wisdom I can offer. So failing that, would you like a cup of tea?"

"That would be lovely."

I was halfway out of the room when she said, "Alexei knew all about her, did I tell you? He asked her about her Russian mother, and the Royal Society, the voles, everything. So she was right, he was just using me to get to her."

"You can't be sure that's true. You've only got her word for it."

"She did it for my sake, she said, she got rid of Alexei to protect me . . . she said the same thing when she fired Sasha's nanny. Whom Sasha loved more than anyone. I just remembered that. And she believes it, she always convinces herself her motives are above reproach, she's blind to anything she doesn't want to see." Suddenly her face contorted, as though in pain. "But maybe I'm the same . . . like with Sasha . . . I didn't see because I didn't want to know. Not wanting to know . . . that's a kind of sin, isn't it?"

"That depends. What is it exactly you didn't want to know?"

She jerked herself upright. "Nothing. I'm just being silly. Morbid. I'd really love some tea."

When I returned, bearing two mugs, she had fallen asleep again, splayed awkwardly across the back of the sofa, her mouth sagging open. Jack's father's blanket had fallen on the floor. I fitted it around her shoulders and maneuvered a battered green cushion carefully under her head. Then I sat at the rolltop desk she'd admired, drinking both mugs of tea in succession, while dawn broke outside the window, pale honey-colored streaks of light just visible over the rooftops. I knew I couldn't sleep—it felt as though something had ended, some long dream I'd been living.

She looked her age; she looked as unglamorous as could be, her face drawn and haggard in the gray light, her skin blotched with tears. For the first time I noticed the faint lines fanning out from her eyes, the softened flesh at her chin.

Once, in the summer before college, my friend Betsy and I bought some acid from one of the leather-jacketed boys at the 7-Eleven, and swallowed the little squares of blotting paper in the woods behind my mother's house. After all the swirls and bursts and explosions of color had faded, and the fits of laughter had stopped; when all the energy had drained away, but my nerves were still alight, everything around me—the clouds, the bark of the maple we lay under, a scruffy mutt who trotted past us, shaking an empty McDonald's box—was suffused with a luminous tenderness; I seemed to be looking into the fragile heart of things, without myself in the way. Something like that feeling was there as I sat watching Isabel with the sky lightening behind her.

She gave a little shiver, moaned slightly, the blanket slipped off her shoulders. Tucking it around her again, I had a sudden image, like a premonition, of the two of us grown old, sitting together in her garden at Sidworth, luxuriating in the sun like two purring cats. We'd be content, peaceful at last, because beyond desire. But of course it was no sort of premonition. She would never grow old, I never saw her again after she left that morning.

Twenty-One

It was Hester who told me, Hester being an avid reader of newspapers, as I was not.

For two days I'd waited for Isabel to phone; for the following three days I'd been dialing her number every few hours and getting her answering machine, leaving increasingly distressed messages. I told myself maybe she was visiting Lucy at Bedales, maybe she'd escaped to her friends' house in the south of France, maybe she'd turned off her phone. But wherever she was, she should have made contact. I felt slighted as much as worried, jealous of whomever she might have turned to instead of me; I wanted her not to need any other comforters.

Adding to my sense of abandonment, Jack didn't phone me either in those five days, and I had lost the right to berate him for it. But I was very much at loose ends; the article on Alexei had been sent off two weeks before, and I was waiting to hear from the editor; in the meantime I had nothing to divert me, except an article on Regency writing boxes that I couldn't even bring myself to start. So I took to the streets.

Spring had burst through with a vengeance, everything so lushly green, the sky so translucently blue, it was impossible to believe in the dreariness of the winter just past. Distracted as I was, I had moments of pure elation among the flowerbeds in Regent's Park, watching the tulips sway in the wind. I could be cheered for whole minutes by a dazzle of purple when the sun reemerged from a cloud, or, on Primrose Hill, a golden retriever wriggling down a slope with a shrieking little boy in a blue coat chasing after.

When I got back to the flat that last day the answerphone was blinking twice—the unwatched pot had boiled, my reward, I felt, for having stopped fretting. The first message was from the editor at *Harper's*: everybody had read my piece, including Lewis, they were enthusiastic, they just had a few questions...could I call him at this number? My pleasure was slightly spoiled by the thought of the good the article might do to Alexei—how everyone who read it would see him as a champion of spiritual truth. But more than that, I was tensing myself, hoping the next voice I heard would be Isabel's. Instead it was Hester's, clipped and strange. "Ring me as soon as you get this, it's urgent."

My first thought, absurdly, was that Jack had told her he'd fallen in love, she was calling to say I should have taken her advice. And so I didn't phone right back; I gathered the pages together, I phoned the guy at *Harper's*, who was in a meeting, and left a message. I made myself a cup of tea, I stood by the window, looking out over the rooftops and thinking of various nasty snide things I could say to Hester when she broke the news of Jack's romance. Then it occurred to me that maybe she had spoken to Isabel, and I picked up the phone and called her.

While she was telling me, I remembered the boy in the blue coat, I remembered the tulips. I stared at the empty sofa, I pressed the receiver tightly to my ear. I saw the leafy street in Richmond, where I'd never been. Even now, I might be shifting gears on University Avenue, or watching a bus roll through the intersection, and there's the blue Citroën, rolling over and over, rocking to a halt with its wheels in the air, though maybe it didn't happen like that at all, maybe there was just one furious explosion, and it was over.

Twenty-Two

G o away," Sasha hissed when she saw me. "Go on, get out of here." And when I didn't, she turned her back on me, or tried to; it's difficult when your leg is in plaster and dangling from the ceiling by a pulley, and a plastic tube, hooked up to a bag of liquid, is attached to your arm, your head is swathed in bandages.

I hovered a few feet away, listening to her fierce pants. Everything in the room was snow white, like Sasha's gown and cast and bandages, except for a bunch of violets drooping from a tooth glass on the white bedstand, and on the windowsill a huge bouquet of glossy yellow roses, so perfect they looked artificial.

"Where's Daphne?" I asked, my eyes returning to the violets.

"Fuck off," she said at the wall.

"Tell me where to find Daphne first."

"Daphne does as she's told. If I tell her to fuck off, she fucks off." She turned her head, giving me a baleful stare. "Who are you, anyway? I don't even know you." And then, before I could answer, "Now I remember. You came with my brother. You're the one who likes dead people."

"I'm a friend of your sister."

"You *were*...you *were* a friend of my sister. Is that why you came? Because you like dead people?"

"No. I wanted to see you."

"To see if I was still alive? Well, I am. I'm going to go on living and living and living. Isn't that a charming thought."

Just then I heard him in the corridor. I hadn't heard his voice in almost three years, but I knew right away. "Perhaps you could find a vase for these," he was saying, being charming.

"Certainly, sir," the nurse said, her tone like a curtsey. "I'll do that for you right away." He had that effect on people.

I shrank back against the wall, and then there he was: his hair was thinner, and his face too; the last traces of boyishness were gone. A worried-looking blonde in a pink linen suit followed him in, clutching her bag in both hands. He nodded curtly at me, without any show of surprise, and then introduced her to Sasha: "This is Anita." She and I went on standing, while he pulled up the chair and sat by the bed. "God, you're a mess," he said, briskly cheerful.

Sasha seemed to shrink too, inside the plaster and the bandages. When she spoke it was in the voice of a little girl. "Don't hate me, Junes. Please. I can't bear it."

"Of course I don't hate you," he said smoothly.

"I keep thinking about Lucy...I thought when she walked in"—she gestured toward me with her unencumbered hand—"she was Lucy. Do you think she'll come? And then she'll say, 'You should have died instead,' and she'll be right. A million million times. The policeman tried to make me say it wasn't my fault, a dog ran in front of the car, or I had a heart attack or something. But I wouldn't say it. I just wanted to go faster and faster, I wanted my head to blast open."

"Never mind that now. Best not to dwell on it."

"I always loved to drive fast. Remember? Remember when Mum gave you her old Rover, and you let me drive it round the park? And you had to grab the wheel and pull it because I almost hit that tree by the pond? Remember that?"

"I'm afraid I don't."

"It was on my birthday . . . you let me drive because it was my birthday. I was thirteen."

"Right . . . I've brought you some flowers. Actually it was Anita's idea. Aren't you even going to say hello to her?"

"Hello," Sasha said, spitting out the word. Anita, twisting a lock of hair around one finger, said she was really sorry about the accident. She sounded very young, younger than she looked. "I just can't imagine . . . it must be so awful," she said helplessly, and trailed off.

Julian shot her a furious look—I knew then she was proving as unsatisfactory as I had been. "You're not here to imagine it."

"And what exactly *is* she here for?" Sasha was trying to sit up; she scrabbled with her bandaged hands, pushing them into the sheets, before sinking down again.

"She came to keep me company. And she wanted to meet you."

"Why? Because you told her what a lovely girl I am? How did you phrase it, Junes? A very lovely girl who killed her sister? Did you say I was barking? Not the full ticket?"

"I really don't recall my exact description."

"There you go again. Julian the unrememberer. The great forgetter. I hope you at least told her about Esme."

"As a matter of fact I didn't."

"Esme was our horse," she said, addressing Anita. "She was supposed to be for all us children. But she was in love with Junes. She used to follow him around, nuzzling his neck, his shoulders, licking his face. Like a dog. Poor Esme. Have you forgotten her too?"

"I can't imagine where that nurse has got to with the flowers."

"Tell her to bring more Demerol while she's at it. Lots of it." She addressed herself to Anita again. "I'm on the most marvelous cocktail of drugs. Pain-killers, tranquilizers, antipsychotics. Are you familiar with fluphenazine? Haloperidol? Get Julian to tell you about the Sunday in the greenhouse. There was a service on the radio, remember, Junes? A sermon about Isaiah. You said you wanted to show me the orchids."

"I have no idea what you're talking about."

"With those little plastic labels on sticks."

"Anyway it was a very long time ago."

"I remember the noise the pots made when you pushed them aside. The crash as they broke on the floor. Poor Mark, Mum blamed him for that. For everything. Every sparrow that fell. But I was the sparrow that day, I was the one that fell." And then to Anita again, "I'm dirty, you see. I'm just dirt."

"Stop it," he said sharply. "Haven't you made enough trouble already?"

A harsh intake of breath; then sobs racked her body, shaking the tubes running into her arm.

"I'm really sorry, I shouldn't have come," Anita said, seeming on the verge of tears herself. She was a nice woman, I could see that. "I'd better go now." She started toward the door. I was just about to follow when Sasha spoke again.

"No," she said, and now her voice was as steely as Julian's; there were no tears in it. "Don't go. I want you to stay and listen. I'll scream if you leave. He knows what that sounds like, don't you, Junes?"

"Stop it," he hissed. "Don't do this."

"I'll tell you something funny, I just sussed it: you've fucked every woman in this room. Isn't that a good joke? Isn't that really quite amusing, when you think about it?"

"I've got to get out of here," Anita said, whimpering. I didn't like her so much then. "I can't listen to this." She click-clacked away on her high heels, I could still hear them out in the corridor.

"You mad bitch."

But Sasha ignored him; she was looking at me. "It was a regular tour of Sidworth"—her voice rising higher and higher, a bat's squeak, a dog whistle, but still the words came clearly. "In the greenhouse, on the bank of the pond, in the woods. Under the oak planted by Grandmother Sasha. On the hay in Esme's stall."

"Shut up." But he sounded frightened now; she had got to him at last. "Liar," he said mechanically, with a quick glance at me. For just that instant I could see him as a little boy, afraid of his mother's power.

"What was I lying about? Esme? But it's true, she loved you to pieces. Julian the irresistible." Her voice grew drowsy; her eyes were starting to close, as though the painkillers were getting to her after all. "You didn't fuck her too, Junes, did you? It doesn't matter. Because she still would have loved you, just like I did . . . But all those places you took me . . . why not just in my room? Mum would never have noticed. Why go tromping through Colley Meadow to the pond? When the bank was so wet . . . it was all mud that day."

"I don't know what you're talking about."

"It was where Mum used to fuck her lovers, wasn't it? All the same places she went. Like getting your revenge."

He rose from his chair, I thought he might hit her, but instead he went to the foot of the bed, clenching and unclenching his fists. "Let it go, Sash. It was a long time ago. Enough damage has been done. I'm going to forget all about it, forget it ever happened, and you'd better do the same. Because otherwise you'll wind up in the bin again, for good this time. Or you'll kill someone else. Is that what you want?"

"Get out," I yelled, "get away from her," but I couldn't be sure he heard me. Sasha was screaming, a wordless howl like an animal in the dark. I headed for him in blind fury, clawing at his face, but deft as always, he grabbed my hands, twisting them over my head. I was struggling to break free when a nurse came pounding in, red-faced, summoned by Sasha's wails. Julian let go of me. "I'm afraid she's terribly distraught," he said, in his most elegant voice. "Only to be expected, I suppose. As you may have heard, she was responsible for the death of our elder sister."

"You bastard," I hissed.

Ignoring Sasha for a moment, the nurse looked from me to him and back again, frankly curious. Then she resumed her professional air.

"I'll have to ask you both to leave. Right now, please."

"Certainly." He went to the door, stopped, turned. "But the flowers I brought for her seem to have disappeared. Perhaps you could track them down."

"I'll do that in a moment, sir. Right now I'm more concerned about the patient." She crossed to the bedside, opening the drawer of the nightstand to extract a vial of liquid and a needle in a paper sheath, though already Sasha's howls were subsiding into whimpers.

"Can I say good-bye to her?" I asked, but the nurse didn't answer, so I said it anyway. Sasha turned her head toward me as the needle went in, and then, suddenly peaceful, she mumbled something I couldn't catch.

Julian was just outside, in the corridor. "She's distorting the facts, of course," he said coolly, matching the rhythm of his steps to mine as I walked toward the lift. I knew he'd been waiting for me, to tell me that. "It wasn't at all the way she said, it was much more her doing. A sort of Lolita scenario, you might say."

He pressed the button, and the doors opened; he stood aside to let me enter, but I went on standing there.

"Aren't you coming? Or are you planning to go back for more?"

I wish now that I'd spat in his face, I wish I'd shouted at him that he was the real killer, if he'd never fucked Sasha Isabel would still be alive. The nurse's station was just opposite; two middle-aged women were laughing about what Ethel had called Dot on *East-Enders*. He would have minded if they'd heard me, he always minded how people saw him.

More than that, though, I wish I'd gone back to Sasha's room. I wish I'd waited for the nurse to leave and then crawled in between the tube and the pulley, as close as I could get, and stroked Sasha's face, and whispered to her, and wiped away her tears. I should have done it for Isabel, it was what she would have wanted. She would never have wanted Sasha to wake up alone.

Instead I headed for the stairs, I ran out on the street before he'd emerged. Then I went back to the flat and dialed Jack's number, to tell him I was coming to join him.

Twenty-Three

It seems we may be returning to the scene of the crime.

Jack has stopped rhapsodizing about the guy at the garage who always gives Sophie a lollipop, or Sam, at the hardware store, who never runs out of any size nail, who can always put his hand on whatever you're looking for, unlike English ironmongers, who apparently have always just run out of the very thing you need. He no longer regales his colleagues with horror stories about England—the constant coverage of the royals in the news, the arrogant twits reigning over the law courts, the infuriating inefficiency: "It's all a myth about the Empire. They couldn't possibly have run an empire, they can't even get the bloody rubbish collected." And everyone but me would laugh appreciatively, not having heard the line a dozen times before.

At some point during our second year here he started obsessively scanning the *New York Times* for the English football scores, ignoring the headlines on the front pages until he had found them. He complained that there was no beauty to American football;

it lacked fluidity, grace, the ball was never in play for long enough; it was a purely commercial enterprise, designed to accommodate the ads that flashed up every quarter hour. His pride in his raccoon hat from Berman Buckskin, and in navigating icy roads in first gear, was no longer expressed so frequently. He began to make himself English breakfasts, with fried tomatoes and mushrooms and bread, and to grumble about the quality of American bacon. One April morning, when dirty drifts of snow still lined our street, he turned to me in bed and asked, "Don't they even have primroses here?"

Now he's talking about bringing Sophie back to Durham to meet what's left of his family. "And then I want to take her to the Lake District and carry her up Haystacks on my shoulders before I'm too old and decrepit to make it." He has to introduce her to the delights of Marmite and chocolate digestives. He doesn't like her watching American television.

"It's a whole different planet, isn't it? My students hardly know the rest of the globe exists." A sweet little freshman asked him the other day what part of Scotland England was in. But what he minds more than anything else is their idea that America won World War II singlehandedly. His father served on the Arctic convoys to Murmansk, one of just two survivors of a U-boat attack; he was given a special medal by the Russians. His uncle, an RAF navigator, was shot down over Germany aged twenty-two, leaving behind a pregnant wife; he has twin cousins who never met their father.

He wants Sophie to know these stories. He hates to think of her learning the American version.

Plus he's suddenly started tracking the crime rate, which keeps rising: 19,000 victims of muggings, shootings, and stabbings this year. A few weeks ago a ten-year-old boy was gunned down two blocks from where we live by a random shooter. Now he's worrying about Sophie living in a country with more guns than people.

So when a job at Warwick was posted in the *Times Educational Supplement*, he decided to apply. Because of his stint at the U, because he's published half a dozen papers since he's been here, and delivered them at half a dozen conferences, he decided his chances were good. Apparently it's down to him and one other guy now. He had an interview on the phone, a conference call with the members of the department, that went very well. He should be hearing pretty soon.

We'll take it from there, he says, we'll make up our minds if and when they offer him the job. But I can see his mind is already made up; it's only mine I'm not sure of. The clouds of glory are gone, only the reality awaits me, and as we know humankind cannot bear very much reality. But then I have an image of Sophie in a school uniform with a crest on its pocket, and plaits, carrying a scuffed satchel like her father's. I remember the lanes and hedgerows of Devon, the stone churches, which I finally got to see, the sense of something ancient in the damp of the air. It only takes the lavender soap from the health food store to bring back the smell of the orchard where Isabel and I were going to sit in our old age. The *Vogue* piece made no mention of her cottage; Lucy must have inherited it; maybe she's living there now, or maybe she's off in Africa digging wells, and there are refugees in Isabel's kitchen. That would be all right too.

I went back to the hospital the day before I flew to Minnesota. In the week since I'd seen her, the thick bandage around Sasha's head had been reduced to a little skullcap fringed with shaven hair. Her cast, released from its pulley, was stretched out flat and neat on the bedclothes. And her face had changed too: the jagged lines were gone from her forehead, her jaw wasn't clenched. Even her skin looked different, minus its angry flush. When she said hello, her voice had none of the shrillness I remembered, or the false brightness. She only sounded sad.

"I've come to say good-bye," I told her. "I'm going back to America."

"That's good, isn't it? Good for you, I mean."

"I think so."

"Oh, yes, I'm sure it is. You couldn't stay here forever," she said kindly, as though she knew all about me, as though we were the best of friends.

"And what about you? What will you do?"

"When I get out of here? I don't know. First I'll go see Lucy, if she'll let me . . . she's in Greece now, she's gone to be with her father's family. Nobody knows when she's coming back. Or if she even will. Did you ever meet her?"

I shook my head. "But I saw her at the funeral. I knew who she was because she looked so much like her mother."

"I think Issy knew, that last day. About Junes. I think she'd figured it out."

"It doesn't matter now," I said, remembering the night at Jack's flat. "I didn't see because I didn't want to know," she'd said . . . "That's a kind of sin, isn't it?"

"But that's why I put my foot on the accelerator. Because I couldn't bear for her to know. I loved Issy better than anyone. But I killed her. So am I better or worse than Junes?"

If the Warwick job comes through, we'll rent a house outside town, Jack says, or even see about buying one. I could have a study, and get down to serious work. And we could plant a garden, with herbs and tulips and pink lilies. Not Eden, but an ordinary English garden, where Sophie, whose curved upper lip is like my father's, can sit on a blanket, in a little striped bonnet, while I weed the borders. We'll get a dog, an old Aga, a climbing rose—Madame Alfred Carrière, who'll flourish without direct sunlight, on a north wall, who'll keep producing white flowers all summer long. Or so she told me once. And every time I look at it, I'll remember.

For the gift of peace and solitude and beautiful surroundings in which to work, I thank the Corporation of Yaddo, the Spiti tis Logotexnias on Paros, the Maison Dora Maar, and the International Writers' and Translators' Centre of Rhodes. My thanks also to Judith Gurewich and Janice Goldklang for their unwavering help and support (and patience), and to Alexandra Poreda and Yvonne Cárdenas for paying such close attention.

Evelyn Toynton's most recent book was *Jackson Pollock*, published by Yale University Press in 2012. Her novel *Modern Art* was a *New York Times* Notable Book of the Year and was translated into Russian; Other Press published her second novel, *The Oriental Wife*, which has been optioned for a film and published in a Greek translation. Her essays, articles, and reviews have appeared in *Harper's*, *The Atlantic*, *American Scholar*, *London Review of Books*, *Times Literary Supplement*, *Salmagundi*, and *Prospect*, among others, and have been reprinted in several anthologies, including *Rereadings*; *Mentors, Muses & Monsters*; and *Table Talk from the Threepenny Review*.